DEATHLY FLOWERS

Adison Black

Verdant Opus
PO Box 342
Lawrence, KS 66044

Edited by Agatha Whitechapel.
Cover art and design by Kyla Love
Interior design by Rachelle Greene

ISBN: 979-8-9995231-0-5
ISBN eBook: 979-8-9995231-1-2

Printed in the United States of America

First Edition October 2025

10 9 8 7 6 5 4 3 2 1

VERDANT OPUS

To those who were told they are not enough, too much, or unworthy—
Put that weight down, it is not yours to carry.

CHAPTER ONE

"Oh, shit!" Tiye screams, shades of green enveloping her senses as she flies face-first into the ground.

Air rushes from her lungs in a painful expulsion. Gasping, she sits up, scanning her surroundings, noting only the dense set of trees around her. *How in the underworlds did I end up here?* she thinks.

The forest air is crisp, thick with the scent of damp earth and something she has never smelled before. Towering trees cast long shadows, and the dim light of dusk makes the forest seem vast and unknowable.

"Well, this sure as shit isn't the dungeons," she says.

CHAPTER TWO

Five months ago …

The worn door of the apothecary closes with a faint click of the lock, a wisp of the herbal scent escaping it wafting into Tiye's nose. She takes a deep breath as the rustle of the last customer's skirts swishes against the sand behind her.

Repositioning the tinctures in her arms, Tiye turns to face a severe scowl, plastering a fake smile on her face. "Sorry, I have to go. I need to deliver these to a customer."

"I hope you did not screw them up like last time," Sitamun says, the callous tone matching her expression.

"That was years ago, Mother."

Tiye's shoulders dip forward as she speeds away from her mother, heading to the old stone tavern at the edge of town. Shaking off the heavy weight of Sitamun's words as she passes the weather-aged sandstone homes that make up most of the small village of Ramses.

Less than three blocks away, Tiye's boot catches, pitching

her flailing forward, tinctures cascading to the ground, glass clinking and bouncing across the sandy street. Her palms slam into the grit on the road, stopping her face from meeting the same fate.

At thirty-four, Tiye hoped she'd outgrow her clumsiness and lack of attention to obstacles in her path, or was it spatial awareness weakness? Or an inability to not bungle? Either way, her overactive imagination seems permanent, so—she now supposes—why should her awkwardness be any different?

Pushing herself up, she scoops the vials back into her arms with the speed of someone used to this kind of disaster. Frowning as she counts the five containers in her hands, she peruses the ground for the final bottle when her eyes fall on a pair of boots. Tiye would recognize those boots anywhere, with the soot clinging to the seams and small burns throughout.

"Still can't stop tripping over your feet to see me?" mocks Senusret. Tall, body built from hours in the forge, he towers over her with a glint in his yellow eyes that even in his human form contain a wolfish gleam.

"Lost my footing when I remembered I was stupid enough to sleep with you," chides Tiye.

The wolf shifter gently dangles the final tincture from his fingertips, swaying it from side to side, as a grin creases his handsome features. Tiye snatches it out of his grip, elbowing him in the ribs good naturedly, and easily sliding past him as she does. Although their friendship had always brought questions because witches tended to have more power and money than shifters in Famsastu, Tiye and Senusret were an inseparable pair.

"There is no need for violence, T. I will always sleep with you again if you just ask," Senusret teases, tucking his brown hair fallen loose from the leather at the nape of his neck, back behind his ear.

"I would not sleep with you again if you were the last person on this goddess-forsaken mound of sand. And stop calling me T; it makes me sound like a child. Did you finally get anything useful this time?"

"You will have to wait to see like everyone else, *Tee*," he says, drawing out his chosen nickname for her. "When you aren't sleeping with me, you don't get the inside scoop," he finishes with a wink.

"You are the worst. I wish a glivner would eat those memories right out of my head," Tiye grumbles, picturing the long skinny, burnt-orange creatures that hid in the sand, waiting to crawl up the leg of an unsuspecting person. Sadly, a person could not choose which memories were taken by a glivner, or she would have used their magic to remove an entire list many moons ago.

))☾((

Her heart sings as the tavern comes into view. The worn stone window ledges feel like home under Tiye's fingers as she begins applying the first of the tinctures to the frame. Warmth floods down her arms from the pulsating power as she infuses protection into the red smoke mixture with her magic. The tincture causes smoke to encase the window should any unwanted observers attempt to spy on a meeting taking place within. Tiye Asudem is a witch, as well as the village embalmer, and her unique blend of magic, combined with her apothecary skills, enables her to create particularly potent tinctures.

With her first task complete, Tiye pushes open the heavy tavern door, sand whipping around her as she cradles the final tinctures in her arms. She drops the small assortment of bottles and jars down on the inside of the bar. Opposite her, Senusret leans back on the only good wooden stool in the

4

place.

Tiye pours the remaining tinctures into the doum juice the rebels will drink before the start of the meeting. Unlike the salve she used on the windows, these cause the drinker to break out in vicious red hives if they have malicious intent towards the rebellion. Soon after Pharaoh Seti was elected twenty years ago, he began providing doum juice to the citizens of the kingdom. It tasted like ass but without it, most would die of dehydration.

Her job done, Tiye peers at the juice, which has now taken on a slightly ochre color. Then, she packs the empty bottles in her bag and walks around the bar to where Senusret is still lounging, talking to Pepi, owner of the tavern. The crocodile shifter took Senusret under his wing when Senusret's parents were killed. Tiye sneaks up behind Senusret and knocks him off his stool. Pepi's chest-length ebony beard quivers as he laughs hard enough to shake the doum juice glasses littering the bar.

"What in the underworlds, Akhir?" exclaims Senusret from his sprawl on the floor.

"You deserved it for messing with me earlier. Also, try to use that name again, and I will cut off your tiny balls." Tiye smirks with a glint in her eye just as the first rebel walks in the door.

CHAPTER THREE

Senusret is already across the tavern, flirting with one of the newer rebel members over in the corner by the time Tiye finishes helping Pepi set out the doum juice.

"That kid moves fast," Pepi mumbles quietly.

"I do not know if I have ever heard you say a more obvious thing in my life," Tiye laughs.

Other than the fact Senusret is thirty-six years old, Pepi's comment is spot on. Tiye bore no ill feelings toward him after their sexual relationship ended; in many ways, both he and Pepi have become family to Tiye; they certainly know more about her than her actual family.

"Did you see the missing poster of the healer?" Tiye asks.

"No, was there a new one up?"

"Yeah, I need to do more, Pepi. I can't stand this stagnancy. It's making my skin crawl."

"Through the thickest mud come the most beautiful flowers. But only if the lotus is willing to bloom," says Pepi sagely.

Air shifts around the tavern as an owl screeches, making a loop above the small group of rebel members. The owl shifts into a person as the group settles into their seats. Nakhtmin, stands stoically at the front of the tavern, their brown eyes maintaining an owlish quality about them as they look around. Their short silver hair contrasts with light brown tunic and pants, the loose linen material the same as most citizens of Famsastu. However, each village tended to dye their linen based on their resources, Ramses light brown from their supply of henna, Khufu light blue from the lapis lazuli, and Zafar light pink from the ochre.

At the age of twenty-seven, Nakhtmin's family lost their native homelands. Pharaoh Seti had the last remaining elkwood trees cut down, claiming they were consuming too much of the land's increasingly limited water. Now at the age of forty-six, Nakhtmin stands before us, the unofficial leader of the ramshackle rebellion.

"Welcome, everyone to our meeting today. It looks like we have lost two more from our numbers," they say. "I know, it can be frustrating not making progress as quickly as we hoped, but we have to be careful. We don't want to get caught like the rebellion group from Khufu."

An image from fifteen years ago flashes across Tiye's mind. The crucified and disemboweled rebel member hung at the edge of town. A rebel group from Khufu had led a protest in the streets of the Royal City after Pharaoh Seti prohibited females from living on their own before the age of thirty-five.

Witnesses claim the group did not even make it into the royal square before they were captured. One member from the group was taken to each of the kingdom's villages, where the royal guards hung them from crosses, cutting their stomachs to let loose their intestines, and leaving them to die slowly. Signs were displayed around their necks stating '*A warning to those who defy Pharaoh Seti's rule, for he speaks the word of the gods'.*

"We have to have something concrete to explore to take him down. But we have to be very careful how we uncover this. That said, today, before we hear from Senusret, we have an important request that could finally allow us to get some traction in this rebellion. As we know, twenty years ago, when Pharaoh Seti was voted in by the people to take over control of our land Famsastu from Pharaoh Eonad, Seti had Eonad, his family and the members of the guard closest to him, executed; few were spared."

The air in the room charges with anger, as people shift in their seats uncomfortably.

"However, we have an informant whose parents were among those few who survived and is currently with the royal guard. Over the last year, the informant has supplied the rebellion with limited information. According to them, the pharaoh is in search of a healer to assist his healer because several healers have gone missing. Are there any healers here willing to take on this task?"

The striking young female Senusret has been flirting with, stands up. Her cheeks flush under warm mahogany skin as she says, "I am a healer; I can do it."

"What is your name, child?" Nakhtmin asks.

"Tawosret. And don't worry, I turned of legal age this year." Tawosret specifies with burning cheeks.

"Thank you, Tawosret. That is very brave of you to take this on." Nakhtmin dips their head in acknowledgement to the eighteen-year-old.

The faces around the room vary from impressed, to shocked, to terrified.

"Underworlds, Senusret, she is half your age," Pepi grunts, leaning in to ensure that Senusret and Tiye are the only ones to hear.

Unfortunately, a full-belly cackle accidentally escapes Tiye, and every eye in the tavern turns in her direction. With all eyes fixed on her, she leans away from Senusret, fixing her face full of poise. "Senusret, this is an important meeting. Tickling me is not appropriate. Also, please refrain from touching me in the future." To solidify the lie, she slides as far away from him as she can on her chair.

Senusret gapes like a wide-mouth fish, pinging his eyeballs between Tiye and Pepi. Pepi, true to form, maintains a poker face, staring ahead.

"Senusret, if you have finished being childish, it is time for you to present the information you obtained this week," Nakhtmin says coldly.

Senusret walks to the front with a little less swagger in his tall hulking form than usual.

"Unfortunately, we have not been able to obtain any information this week. We need another set of eyes to keep watch when we are sneaking around during the supply runs to the Royal City," he says.

Tiye hops up, squeaking, "I will do it!"

"Great," Senusret says sarcastically. "Our next supply pick-up is the middle of next week." He then walks back to sit—pointedly—at the table with the young healer.

The room is focused on Nakhtmin, except for Senusret, who sticks his tongue out at Tiye. She chuckles quietly in her seat.

"That concludes our meeting today," Nakhtmin says. "Next week's meeting will be at the same time and place."

The rebel members file out of the tavern, and Nakhtmin, catching Tawosret's attention, motions for her to stay. They talk quietly near the entrance and Senusret settles himself back down at the table with Tiye and Pepi. They lull into an easy conversation, waiting for Nakhtmin and Tawosret to join them. Pepi gathers the empty glasses around the tavern, placing them back behind the bar. He returns with fresh ones for their group and a bowl of sweet sticky dates. Tiye's favorite. She immediately dives into the bowl, popping a date into her mouth and closing her eyes as she chews the sweet-savory fruit.

The hinges of the tavern door screech open as a new face enters. She is unlike anyone Tiye has ever seen. Her long dark hair is secured in a plait down her back, bringing out the color of her creamy skin, and her almond-shaped eyes shine an unnatural shade of violet, so bright they pierce the tavern. Tiye is rooted to the spot, transfixed by the beautiful woman.

"Quit drooling, Tiye." Pepi leans over to whisper. "You know I don't care who you date, but watch yourself with that one. She is part of the royal guard." He gives Tiye a knowing look.

"Damn, girl, when was the last time you got laid? You look like you are in heat over there," chided Senusret from her other side.

Both Senusret and Pepi know Tiye enjoys the company of both males and females; however, they also know the dangers. The laws established under Pharaoh Seti enforce the restriction of marriage between only males and females of the same species. Senusret jumps up, his confidence back as he moves across the room. Snapping out of her shock, Tiye follows behind to join the group.

"Everyone, this is Nebetah. Our informant," Nakhtmin says.

"Hello, it is nice to meet all of you," Nebetah begins, " I've been tasked with finding and coordinating an introduction between an assistant healer and the pharaoh's primary healer, Kek. Nakhtmin, have you been able to find someone willing to do this?"

"Yes," Nakhtmin indicates, "Meet Tawosret."

"Wonderful, you will be assigned to work with Kek. He

has always served the pharaoh and is deeply loyal. Just do whatever he asks and do not try to investigate. Remember any information that you happen to hear through your daily tasks there. Do not write anything down; only report back what you can remember."

"But I thought you wanted me to be a spy?" Tawosret bleats, her expression sulky.

"Absolutely not. You are not trained to be a spy. It is extremely dangerous for you to be there in the first place. Seti is overly suspicious of everyone and you well know his reputation for killing anyone he suspects of being against him, without any verification. Just do the tasks Kek asks you to do. If you happen to hear good information while you're there, make a mental note of it and bring it back. We are just trying to get you integrated into the pharaoh's employment. Once you've been established, we will send in an actual spy."

Disappointment encapsulates Tawosret's face, but she nods anyway. "When do I start?"

"I will contact you once a date has been set for you to meet with Kek." Before Nebetah turns to face Nakhtmin, she gives Tiye an appraising look. "Nakhtmin, I must leave, but I will be back soon."

After watching Nebetah walk out the tavern door, Tiye turns back to the conversation.

"Tiye, we need to brush up on your fighting skills before next week's run because we all know you are too clumsy to be the spy." Senusret scrunches his brow as he ponders the thought.

"Oh, fuck you, Senusret," Tiye announces, rolling her eyes.

At the curse, Tawosret gasps, looking as though she might faint.

Tiye rolls her eyes. "Good Goddess, you'll be the worst spy ever. Senusret, you should focus on training this one to fight." Tiye looks once more toward the tavern door.

CHAPTER FOUR

The remaining members disperse upon the conclusion of the meeting after which, Tiye and Senusret slowly trudge back into town.

"Seriously, Sen, you need to teach Tawosret some basic self-defense ... Immediately," Tiye says.

Teaching Tiye to fight was how Senusret had first grown on her. When Tiye was younger, she was sent to the schoolhouse in her village, where she was taught essential reading and writing with all the other children. Beginning at age ten, the males would get a reprieve in the afternoon from learning basic homemaking skills and instead, were taught to fight. Tiye could not understand why she could not be taught to fight. Upon asking the headmistress as much, she was given ten lashings for her 'insolence.' This was a typical punishment that most, if not all, children received at least once during their schooling. Once was enough for the majority to learn. However, Tiye tended to require punishing at least once a week for her clumsiness, questions, or general inattention. Therefore, on that day, when Senusret found Tiye on her walk home, he was not surprised to learn she had been punished that day. Upon finding out why, he'd offered to teach Tiye himself.

Without Senusret's instruction and their continued practice, Tiye would not be the expert swordsman she is today.

"Oh, I already have it scheduled." Senusret winks.

"You're incorrigible."

"You're the one who gave me the idea. When are you going to have Nebetah *teach you to fight*?" Senusret practically doubles over with mirth.

"I have more important things to worry about than a relationship. Unlike you, I do not go around like a werewolf in heat, fucking anything that stands still long enough in my presence."

"What can I say? I like to keep active." Senusret smirks. "Oh yeah, your birthday is tomorrow. Do you still have the deal with the shopkeeper for the room above the apothecary?"

"Yeah, but I can tell he is growing impatient holding it for me." Tiye hadn't yet met the conditions of living without her parents. She wasn't married, her parents still lived, and she wasn't thirty-five yet. She found ways around living with her parents every day, but it was exhausting. Her birthday couldn't come soon enough.

"But it's been two days since the last shifter moved out?"

"Yes, but you know Trenko. I am sure I'll get to work tomorrow to find out he's rented it out again."

The melodies of flies fill the empty village square, as the pair stop in their usual spot. Senusret hands over a dagger from his boot to Tiye, pulling another from his hip. Squaring her shoulders, she hurls the dagger, needing a release from the tension coursing through her body. The dagger clumsily ricochets off the metal statue of the pharaoh. Age has dulled its shine but the scuffs and scratches are from Tiye and Senusret's weekly routine of throwing daggers at it for the last ten years.

"You know, I remember the day Seti started his campaign. The elkwood trees were dying, and the rainfall was decreasing each year. But then he came to the village announcing he had the solution to the kingdom's increasing problem, the doum palm trees only *he* could provide. He told us he was the new prophet of the gods, that they'd told him if he were to become the next pharaoh of Famsastu, they'd provide enough trees to replace the decreasing water supply with juice from the fruit." Tiye turns on the spot, the memory bringing her rage to the surface. "I was standing in this exact spot with my mother, as she looked upon Seti and said, 'There is a man worthy of being pharaoh. A man who provides what the people of the kingdom need.' It stuck with me. I never could understand why he had to be the pharaoh for the gods to provide for the kingdom's people. And now that he is, things are worse than ever. Each day, more and more healers go missing."

"It didn't help that during the campaign, Eonad became more scatterbrained by the day. Remember all the slogan typos?" Senusret grimaces. "We all suspect he is a false prophet, but who can prove that?"

"I have to do it. Every day I wake up I am reminded how under his rule I am somehow not good enough to even live on my own. How I'm not allowed to love freely. I cannot standby and do nothing anymore," Tiye puffs as she throws the dagger, hitting the statue's leg instead of its chest. "I have to take him down." Grabbing the dagger out of Senusret's hand, she puts all her rage into the throw. "And his laws." The dagger misses the statue completely, landing in the sand a foot away. *Maybe then I can find what is missing in me,* she thinks.

Senusret remains uncharacteristically tactful during this moment of soul-scorching.

The silence makes the feeling of wanting to crawl out of her own skin unbearable to Tiye and she tells him, "Sen, I just want to be alone."

Handing him back his daggers, she turns in the direction of her parents' house.

"You're not sleeping at the apothecary tonight?" Senusret calls.

"No, not tonight."

CHAPTER FIVE

The butterflies in Tiye's stomach wake her early the following day. She takes great care to tie her hair back in an immaculate plait, picking out the best pair of trousers and tunic she owns for her trip to the Royal City. She has only been one other time in her life, and she was so young she barely remembers it. At the age of three, a child born to magical parentage is required to submit to a blood test before the royal guards for official documentation of one's magical ability. However, the vivid memory still remains …

Watching as the blood drops from the spot the guard pricks on her finger, falling to the smooth silver surface below, where it turns into crimson smoke, wafting into the air to form the most breathtaking flowers. The guard as he waves the papyrus through the red smoke, transfixing the smoke forms onto the page …

Cleaning the last of the smudges off her boots until her hands are aching, Tiye finally pulls them on. She sets out to catch the passenger carriage for its singular round trip to the

Royal City it makes each day. Despite how early she has woken up, Tiye is now running late; she begins sprinting to ensure she'll make it on time. Sand slips beneath her as she runs. Sliding around the last corner, her heart slows, finding a line of people still waiting to take their seats in the carriage. Fortunately for Tiye, few people are heading into the Royal City today, and she is directed to a cart with only one person in it.

Tiye's mouth goes dry when she realizes too late that the other occupant is none other than Merneptah. Her back stiffens. The thought of spending the hour-long carriage ride with an ass like him forces her teeth to grind. *I couldn't even luck out to have a single buffer*, she thinks.

As if on cue, Merneptah opens his mouth, "You should have been honored when I asked your parent's permission to marry you. It is the responsibility of the female to be subservient."

"And to the dismay of all parties involved, except me, I vehemently refused," Tiye bats back, "Can we just travel in silence?"

At the last moment, before the carriage takes off, another person climbs gracefully into the cart. Eyes bouncing between Tiye and Merneptah, the young healer chooses the seat next to Tiye. Finding herself with the unlikeliest of travel companions, Merneptah and Tawosret, Tiye balks as the carriage begins to roll forward.

Now, these two would make a perfect couple, she thinks to herself. Tiye resists the urge to say something snarky, instead choosing to look out the window silently at the endless sand stretching out before her. She watches the witch at the front of the carriage whip her hands into the air, the wind rustling the sand, gently pushing the cart forward.

Famsastu is desert land; trees are scarce because water resources are limited. However, it was not always entirely a desert; twenty-five years ago, the lush forest that swept through Famsastu began dying off, and soon after, the rains stopped. Nowadays, it only rains once a year, yet the lightning storms increase almost weekly. These storms are truly perilous to be caught in, but when the lightning hits the sand, it creates sandmar, a metal-like material. Everything that was wood has been replaced by the sandmar.

Tiye adjusts in her seat, trying to find a comfortable position but her sturdy thigh slips off the cushion, jerking from the zap zinging through her leg. The sandmar is forged by metal witches into structures and other items the citizens need and, although the material is extremely useful, it's uncomfortable to sit on as it maintains minute elements of charge from the lightning.

Half an hour later, the carriage screeches to a halt, and Tiye is on the verge of thanking her lucky stars the ride is over when a booming voice demands all passengers exit the carriages.

"As the only male in this carriage, I will exit first to ensure it is safe," Merneptah declares, hopping up.

"Fine by me. Get yourself killed first too, that way when you die we can use your body as a shield," Tiye quips.

"Oh my, do be careful! I would hate for you to die on our account," Tawosret exclaims.

Tiye whips her head round to take in Tawosret at her side. She catches a look on Tawosret's face for just a second, but then it is gone as quickly as it appeared. Unable to interpret the expression, Tawosret's face now holds bulging eyes, mouth flat and unmoving. *Weird.*

Caught off guard by Tawosret's actions, Tiye is not aware that Merneptah has already moved around her to exit the carriage and belatedly moves to stand next to him. He is, to only Tawosret's assumed relief, not dead.

Eyes blinking to adjust to the direct light of the sun, Tiye recognizes the royal guard uniforms as they move down the line of passengers, questioning them as they go. By the time the guards make their way down to where Tiye stands, Tawosret's body is eerily still despite the nervousness on her face.

"Who among you is a healer?" the taller of the two guards closest to the carriage passengers demands.

"I am, sir," Tawosret states, her cheeks burning again.

Tiye wonders if this girl ever stops blushing.

"What is your name?"

"Tawosret Anetha of Ramses, sir. Is something wrong, sir?" she trills tremulously.

Another guard searches through the books they brought with them. When he finds the page he is looking for, he hands the open book to the guard who spoke.

"You look too old to be Tawosret of Ramses," the guard accuses, frowning.

"Oh no, is my year of birth wrong in the book? I just turned of legal age this year," she flusters trying to get a look at the book. "Eighteen."

Huh, thinks Tiye. *She really does not look* that *young*.

The guard pulls the book away from Tawosret, tucking it away in his bag.

"She speaks the truth. I am Merneptah Koob of Ramses. Tawosret grew up in our village; however, many years junior to me and Tiye here," Merneptah states pompously.

"Tiye Asudem here," Tiye says, waving her hand halfheartedly.

"Fine," the guard states. Then, turning to the entire line of passengers, he yells, "We are done here! Get loaded back into your carriages and on your way immediately."

"What is this all about?" Tiye questions the guard.

"Never you mind," the guard growls before walking away.

Still seeing only sand in every direction, Tiye clenches her jaw, her teeth grinding together as she does as she is told.

CHAPTER SIX

The rest of the journey concludes without any further interruptions. Tiye has a barrage of questions she wants to ask Tawosret, but not with Merneptah around. However, the moment she steps out of the carriage, they are wiped from her mind.

Sunlight bounces off the artistically crafted golden sandmar buildings looming over her head, and the posters covering the outside of the buildings in stark contrast overwhelm her eyes. Even twenty years after the election, the pharaoh election campaign signs twisting people's fear of each other's differences, and exploiting those secret, tucked-away feelings of dislike for anyone who does not look or act like themselves, still smother the buildings like scarlet fever. On top are newer posters stating, 'Pharaoh Seti made Famsastu *gloryus!*'

"Sure, you cannot spell glorious, but it is way better now," Tiye mumbles sarcastically under her breath.

"What did you say?" Tawosret trills delightfully, walking up next to her.

"Nothing, don't worry about it," Tiye answers shortly. "Well, I am heading off. See you later." She turns to escape the torturingly sad look on Tawosret's face. *Underworlds, what is with this girl?*

Tiye joins the fray of people moving into the Royal City. Single-story sandstone buildings sprinkled in between the sandmar ones. Street merchants line the streets selling an assortment of items. Sheaths of linen in a bright array of colors hang from booths. Each sheath or kalasiris is intricately stitched with elegant designs of lotus or other various symbols of the gods and goddesses. Others are filled with carts of juicy ripe dates and figs, and the pungent smells of sizzling lamb and crisping parathas waft through the air.

The buildings block any clearly designated path to the courthouse, and Tiye asks one vendor selling seismic mounds of Zalabya for directions. Upon realizing she was not going to buy anything, his sugary attitude turns to utter annoyance.

"Why are you wasting my time?" he says testily before tersely giving her hurried directions.

Tiye sets out in the direction he gave, hoping he did not give her bad directions out of spite.

A knot is forming in her stomach as she takes the final corner, sandstone buildings with metal roofs closing in on her. The busyness of the place, initially so breathtaking, is fast becoming overwhelming. She is debating turning back when she reaches the end of the road. It opens into a large city square, lively with people, and the courthouse stands out against the golden sandmar edifices on either side. Limestone columns in the shape of the goddesses: Isis, Bastet, Hathor, and Sekhmet decorate its front. Standing three stories high, most exclusively in the center is a statue of Ma'at, the goddess of truth, justice, balance, and most importantly—

order.

Glued to the spot, taking in the view of the cosmic female with her scales and feather, Tiye mutters, "Wow." She notices the plaque at the base of the statue, stating it was constructed to signify that the courthouse would honor the goddess with rulings made inside the building. Since Pharaoh Seti has been elected, these rulings have become a mockery of Ma'at's guidance.

Under Pharaoh Eonad's rule, females were seen as equals to their male counterparts. Worshipers revered the gods and goddesses equally, but Pharaoh Seti's guiding campaign focused on returning the lands to the origins of religion and to the gods the people 'should' be worshiping by twisting the grimoires text to fit his agenda.

Tiye launches up the steps of the courthouse with a lightness about her she has not felt in years. An opulent set of wooden doors that have maintained their beauty despite being weathered by sand hide the entrance. The smooth wood slides fluidly out of her hand as she steps inside.

Stopping in her tracks, Tiye's eyes widen as she takes in the hustle and bustle of activity. She watches as papers fly overhead, each finding its intended recipient, as hordes of witches and shifters all walk with purpose throughout the interior of the building as they complete their business.

Across the considerable foyer, Tiye spots Nebetah, her violet eyes squeezing shut as she laughs with another royal guard. Before she can think better of it, she surges forward in her direction, working her way around the room toward the Administrative Petition window, where two individuals are already in line: an elderly witch and a male who looks to be a few years younger than Tiye. Each is identifiable by the sigils tattooed on the backs of their left hands, just like Tiye's. Tiye's hand shows the image of Isis standing, wings outstretched wide, blades in her hands at her side, and the full moon resting atop her head. She looks down upon it now as the elderly witch hobbles up to the window. It opens to reveal a teller.

"Prick your finger and state your purpose," the teller calls through the gap.

"I am here to file my petition to live on my own. My husband just passed away," croaks the elderly witch. Her hand quivers as she jabs her finger on an objectionable-looking spike attached to the ledge of the teller's window.

A moment passes as the teller's hands move lazily back and forth in front of her, before coming to a stop.

"Ma'am, according to our records, your husband passed away a week ago. Unfortunately, you only had three days to file your petition. Since our records show you do not have any other living family members, and you failed to show your competence by submitting the petition within the required timeframe, you will immediately become a ward of the kingdom." She continues soullessly despite the witch's strangled gasp. "You will be remanded into custody straightaway, and a guard will retrieve your necessary items from your house to bring to the sanctuary at Brimstone," the teller states in a dry dulcet tone.

"Please, I beg of you, do not send me there!" the elderly witch cries as two royal guards storm forward, seizing both of her arms and slamming brimstone bracelets around each of her wrists.

The moment the bracelets close, the fire that had begun to form in the witch's palms is immediately snuffed out. The guards lead the sobbing witch out of the atrium and through an innocuous back door. It slams shut behind them with a booming sound, cutting off her cries.

It takes only seconds for the hustle and bustle to resume after its momentary pause, people watching the spectacle turn away. Tiye forces herself to look at the floor, trying to give herself time to contain the rage written all over her face. After several deep breaths, she looks up and moves forward in line behind the male witch, who has now taken his place before the teller's window.

"Prick your finger and state your purpose," the teller carries on as if nothing happened.

"Yes, I would like to file a petition for divorce. My wife is not living up to her wifely duties," the male posits.

"Yes, I see. You have been married for less than one year and have not chosen to settle yet. Excellent." The teller catches the papers as they cascade into the window, handing them to the male. "Please present these to your wife within one week from today. Upon her receipt, your divorce will be finalized. She will have two days to take up residence with her remaining parent or file a petition herself to live on her own."

"Thank you," the male states, smiling as he walks away to exit the courthouse.

It's Tiye's turn.

"Prick your finger and state your purpose," the teller drawls once more.

Tiye stops attempting to bore holes in the male's back with her eyes, steps forward and mutters, "What an ass."

"I may be blind, but I am not deaf, young lady. Watch your manners. Now prick your finger and state your purpose," the teller scolds.

"How can you stand that? What these laws do to females."

"I am here to do a job, that's it. I am just trying to do my job."

Tiye stabs her finger on the spike, the fuming indignation superseding any pain. Breathing deeply to calm her nerves, she states, "I am here to petition my right to live on my own."

"You understand that after a year, if you are still unmarried, you will be forced to settle."

"Yes, I understand."

"Well, if you feel you must. Let's see here." The teller launches her fingers over the raised dots that appeared after the spike was given its blood. "It appears you have been saved from your choices, at least for one day. Your birthdate is not until tomorrow."

"That cannot be right; my birthdate is today, the tenth," Tiye says, grasping for certainty.

"I know it is difficult without a male to help guide you, but your birthdate is the eleventh. See here," the teller says, catching a scroll that flew up behind her, smoothing it out on the counter between, pointing at the date for Tiye to see. The date clearly states the eleventh of the month, with her parents' signatures unmistakably below it. "Let this be your lesson and your guide to investing in finding you a match," the teller says. "Next!"

Someone pushes past her, her legs moving of their own accord as her body guides her to the courthouse exit. Thoughts of Nebetah are gone as her brain wades through a fog of confusion. Being jostled this way and that by passersby hastily pushing past her to their next thing, Tiye pivots into an alleyway off the square to escape the bustle and bodies overwhelming her senses. The further she walks, the more the muted sounds and clear pathways help to clear the haze from her mind. Looking around, Tiye finds herself in a quiet, empty alleyway without any familiar landmarks nearby, turning in a circle for anything that might give her a direction back. *Is this where the warehouse is for the supply run?* she wonders.

A scream rents the air, wrenching her gut, and she sprints in its direction, to the cross section of the alleyway, searching for the owner. Coming to the end of the building, she skids to a halt, registering that she does not have a weapon, should she need one. Slowly, she peers around the corner. Her heart drops as her eyes force her brain to acknowledge what she is seeing.

The elderly witch from the courthouse is on her knees, trembling as she pulls at the chains secured low on each wall of the narrow alleyway. Chains force her to kneel while the same guards stand behind her. The shorter guard hastily secures a cloth over her mouth, muffling her cries, before backing away. Abruptly, the taller of the two swiftly slices his khopesh level with the elderly witch's neck.

For a moment, Tiye thinks the guard missed or is playing some sort of sick joke, but a moment later, the elderly witch's entire body freezes, the muted screams stopping entirely as her head slips from her shoulders, blood spurting from the body as it slumps forward. Tiye's hand trembles as she throws it over her mouth to prevent any sound escaping her lips.

"Hurry up, get the heart. I want to get this over with," says Guard One.

"Why do I always have to do this bit? It always gets my uniform dirty. If Kek needs these hearts so bad, why doesn't he do it himself?" Guard Two whines.

"You know this, I kill them, you collect the hearts. Orders are orders. Hurry up, her scream could have attracted attention."

Guard One's head lifts in the direction of the alleyway where Tiye is spying. She whirls, throwing herself back, and slamming into the wall, holding her breath as her own heart hammers. The clink of metal and ripping of fabric meet her ears.

"Hey, go check the alleyway," Guard One says, "I thought I saw something."

Shit, shit, shit, runs through Tiye's head.

"Do you want me to do this or that?" Guard Two is having a multiple choice day.

Tiye doesn't wait. She takes off, sprinting down the alleyway, her head whipping back and forth, looking for a place to hide. Heart pounding, air filling only the top half of her lungs, she sees a break in the wall. Running headlong around the corner, her legs almost turn to water as she is met with a bustling street. People. *Witnesses.* Slowing herself to a quick walk, Tiye secures her scarf over her hair as she finds a spot on the adjacent wall to post herself. Leaning against the wall with quaking legs, she slows her breaths to loosen the hold the lightheadedness has on her.

Not a minute later, and the first guard pokes his head out of the alleyway, looking around the market. Scanning the area twice and seemingly satisfied no one witnessed them after all, he slips back into the alleyway and out of sight.

Tiye waits in the same spot, waiting for her legs and hands to quit their shaking, before a merchant brings his sheath skirts decorated with jewels over to show her. Unsure of what might come out of her mouth, Tiye shakes her head mutely. Walking away, she makes her way back to the carriages. It takes her so long to find the right route, but she is still afraid to open her mouth for directions; it takes her double the amount of time to get back to the carriage station.

As she arrives, they are making the last call.

Loading up, she finds herself once again in the same carriage as Merneptah and Tawosret, who is chattering away to apparently anyone who will listen. Tiye closes her eyes as the carriage shifts forward on its trek back to the village. She sits silently for the entire ride, lost in thought, an unswallowable lump caught in her throat.

Later, Tiye wonders what Tawosret spent her afternoon doing in the Royal City.

Upon arriving back at Ramses, Tiye steps off the carriage still lost in thought until she finds herself face to face with her mother, anger radiating from every pore.

CHAPTER SEVEN

"How dare you go into the Royal City to request that disgraceful petition!" Sitamun hisses.

"Mother, can we please discuss this at home?" Lowering her head, Tiye dashes past, heading for the least populated route to her parent's home. *Goddess, can she just once not make a scene?* Tiye thinks to herself.

Spying Senusret walking up to the carriage with a small package in his hand, Tiye's stomach clenches and, not wanting him to be subjected to her mother's wrath, she swiftly changes direction. Turning a corner, placing a house between Senusret and her mother's line of sight, she takes a turn along the next row of houses before doubling back in the right direction again.

"You are such an insolent brat! This is about that sand-spawn boy, isn't it?" Sitamun spits, catching up.

Thank the Goddess she did not see him, Tiye reflects. Red filling her vision, Tiye spins on her heel so quickly her mother almost runs into her. "Do not call him that, and this has absolutely nothing to do with Senusret," she spits back, venom lacing her words. Before it can escalate and become a screaming row, Tiye walks away. *Not today.*

Undeterred by Tiye's outburst, the grainy swish of her mother's skirt catches and releases the ground as she follows behind her daughter.

"Ever since you met him, you've become a different person. You were such a well-behaved child, and after you met him, you became moody and angry. Everyone in the village notices; that's why Merneptah's parents encouraged him to request your hand in marriage. And look how your irrational behaviors have ruined that opportunity; you could have been the wife to the wealthiest witch in Ramses!"

Keeping quiet, Tiye hurries to her parent's house, knowing anything she says will be turned against her and only further deteriorate her mother's already terrible mood. After experiencing this behavior her entire life, Tiye has become accustomed to the impulses of Sitamun's tempers. Learning to say as little as possible and supplicating herself to Sitamun tended to be the only thing that lessened the duration and voracity of the tantrums.

A traitorous kernel of a wish that blossomed—to be comforted by her mother—soured in Tiye's chest. *What is wrong with me that I let myself hope for her to change?* Tiye wonders.

She drags herself through the front door of her parent's house with her mother hot on her heels, still berating her about all the ways she is an embarrassment, not only to Sitamun, but to the entire family. Her mother moves past her and Tiye turns, the heavy weight on her shoulders lessening slightly as she blocks out the rest of the world, shoving the door shut.

"As if it's not bad enough that you refuse to dress like a

proper female, you take no pride in your appearance. Just look at your hair and those boots! Did you even attempt to shine them before going out to embarrass everyone?"

It continues …

"Whas going on here?"

The scent of alcohol fills the space before Tiye sees him, her father, glowering from across the room and waiting for the answer.

"Your daughter has decided to spend her birthday embarrassing our entire family by gallivanting off to the Royal City to request a petition to live on her own," Sitamun says.

"How-how dare you!" Thutmose booms as he wheels to face her, straightening (with some wobble) to his full height, filling even more of their modest living space.

Fury causes her to break her silence, and Tiye speaks with clenched fists, "Do you want to explain why the records in Royal City state my birthdate is tomorrow?"

"You know this: the clerics refuse to correct the record. And gods, that test showed you had so much potential, but you have failed to live up to it," Sitamun says, shaking her head.

Her false simpering tone sets Tiye's skin on edge. "Why in the underworlds would I remember that?"

Suddenly, her father's eyes narrow on her. "Where exactly did you get the money to pay for a carriage ride into the Royal City?" he asks.

A chill went through her as she lies, "I saved it from my earnings last week."

SMACK! Tiye's head snaps to the side from the impact of her father's palm across her face.

She stills. Her father's anger rarely turns physical, unlike her mother's, who wields her presence and words like weapons.

"What else have you stolen from this family?" he demands. "Search her room for anything else, Sitamun"

His lips press into a hard mean line as he continues to tower over her while her mother scurries off to Tiye's room. Within seconds of her disappearing through the doorway, the noise of items being tossed bangs out of her room, reverberating in her ears. After another minute, Sitamun stalks back into the room with heavy footfalls, shaking her head in silent answer.

"Go to your room and stay in there until you leave for the apothecary tomorrow. You will ask for extra shifts to make up for the money you wasted today. This is why we have supported Pharaoh Seti and his agenda since the beginning: you need to learn your place," Thutmose says.

Tiye walks in the direction of her room, she holds her head high despite her still smarting cheek. Spotting her brother, Teti, she moves past him wordlessly. He won't help; he never does.

I don't understand how I am still dealing with this shit as an adult. Even if I can get out soon, I cannot continue to let others fall to fates like these due to Seti's laws.

Under his breath as she passes, Teti asks, "Why do you always insist on riling them up?" His gold eyes, almost indistinguishable to Tiye's, narrow in annoyance.

Despite the similarities in their appearances, from their heights to the bronze of their skins, Tiye and Teti's personalities could not be more different. As the older sibling, Tiye always guarded Teti from their parents' erratic behaviors during their childhood. As they grew older and became adults, Tiye hoped Teti would stand with her, but he has yet to do so.

Behind the safety of her door, Tiye finally lets a single tear track down her face before she sets to undo the upheaval of her room.

CHAPTER EIGHT

After a fitful night of sleep, the dark presses around her as Tiye walks down the empty streets of Ramses. The village is filled with the low creaking of sandmar roofs straining to remain in place against the pull of the wind. Tiye longs to see the thatched roofs of her childhood; all of which were confiscated and burned by the kingdom 'for the betterment of the villages.' Now they are just corrugated sandmar panels. While the gold of the sandmar brought an elegance to their sleepy village, Tiye aches for the connection to nature that has dwindled way.

The sand slips effortlessly below her boots while her mind drowns in thoughts, but the familiar groan of the apothecary door silences the tumult in her head. Its earthy smells bring a calming salve to her frayed nerves. Readying the workbench with her favorite mortar, pestle, and blade, Tiye finds the scratched list of orders placed yesterday. Setting to work, she relaxes bit by bit, as her mind dives into the tasks that lie before her.

The sun is fully present in the sky when Senusret walks into the shop, breaking Tiye's concentration for the first time since she set to work. Working into the early hours of the morning, she has kept her hands busy to stave off thoughts of yesterday. She is surprised when Senusret places a package on the workbench before her, as she sets aside the last of a completed order.

"What is this? Shouldn't you be at the forge?" she asks him.

"Yeah, but I wanted to drop this off for you personally, since I didn't get to yesterday. Your mother looked pissed. You know, I know how she gets, I just did *not* want to add that."

"Oh. Yeah, she was pissed, but it's just the usual 'You're a disgrace to this family' nonsense. My father is the one who is angrier because I stole from the fam—" Tiye freezes, her hands still holding open the edges of the wrappings, transfixed by the beautifully inlaid dagger nestled in the stained fabric. "What is *this*?"

"Don't get all sentimental. I just wanted to give you a dagger of your own to celebrate this milestone."

Tiye's heart stops, fear flooding her veins as her eyes shoot wide. *Oh no, this* cannot *be happening. I* cannot *lose Sen as a friend. Shit, did I do something to mislead him?*

Without warning, Senusret cackles, doubling over with laughter. "The look on your face is priceless. Tiye don't overthink this. I know I made a lot of jokes about us in the past, but they are just jokes. You are my best friend, that's all. If it would help ease your mind, I was making one for Tawosret, and this was my first attempt."

Laughter lights his face as memories of yesterday flood back to Tiye.

"Well, thanks, Sen, but I-you will have to hold on to this

for me, for the time being," she gets out.

Confusion fills Senusret's features, morphing into melancholy as Tiye explains the events in the courthouse yesterday.

"So now, I don't know when I will have another chance to take the carriage into the Royal City to seek the petition again. You know my mother will be staking out the carriage station for at least the next week to make sure I don't try it again. Are you okay still holding onto my coin?"

"Of course I can," Senusret says easily. "Tiye, I am sorry about your birthdate and being stuck with your parents. Maybe on the supply run, you can stop at the courthouse; it's not far from where we pick up the supplies. Sure as shit, your mother will *not* be staking out the supply run stables or carts."

The events of yesterday drive Tiye's new mission for a rebellion from her head. Feeling refreshed, she crashes around the workbench, slamming Senusret into a crushing hug. "Are you sure the rest of the group won't mind?"

"Nah, they won't care," he says.

"Oh, thank you! I have to tell you about something else that happened yesterday."

Senusret's eyebrows rise until they disappear below his shaggy brown hair as Tiye describes the scene in the alleyway, his yellow eyes popping when she finally finishes.

"Damn, Tiye, are you sure you're okay?" he asks, eliciting a nod from her before he continues, "You need to tell Nakhtmin about what you saw. Underworlds, Kek is a sick fuck. You are so lucky they didn't see you." He hugs her once more, asking as he releases her, "You sure you're okay?"

It didn't happen to you. You're fine. Pull it together, Tiye scolds herself as she nods, smiling up at him. "Of course I'm fine. Stop hovering."

"See you at Pepi's later, then?" he asks as he slides out the door.

"I wish. Not tonight. I need to keep a low profile. I'll make sure to tell them as soon as I can, though. Thanks again, Sen, for the dagger. It is beautiful."

"Anytime. Oh, and happy real birthday, Tiye."

))◐((

Not long after Senusret leaves, Sitamun walks into the apothecary. Cane in hand, she makes her way to her workbench, face contorted into a pity-seeking expression.

Tiye's back straightens. *Don't get sucked in,* she tells herself.

"Tiye, darling. Yesterday did not go as I intended …"

Tiye squeezes the handle of her paring knife hard enough that the wood gives a slight moan and Sitamun eyes the knife with apparent concern. Releasing her grip, Tiye sets it down with her other tools on the workbench.

"Ah, much better. You see, Tiye, the reason I am so hard on you is because you represent our family. What you do and how you dress," her lip curls as she looks over Tiye's outfit reproachfully, covered in herbs and stains, "represents our status as a family within the village. Just as I was taught by my parents, I teach you and your brother the responsibilities that come with representing our family."

Tiye bites the inside of her cheek to keep quiet.

"You see, I do this for you. To make you better. I understand it may seem unfair that your brother has fewer rules to follow, but that is the burden we bear as females. You should really be grateful that I am not like *my* mother," Sitamun enthuses. "*She* required me to braid my hair so tightly my scalp bled, and I would have to polish my shoes for hours every day until she was satisfied with my appearance. Even then, there would always be something wrong." She pauses, her eyes have a distant look in them as she seems to consider her own upbringing.

Then her hands find Tiye, and she sweeps stray hairs that have fallen loose from Tiye's braid back out of her face. Tiye stands stock still, resisting the urge to lean into the touch or flinch. Her nerves teeter on the edge, threating to fall into sorrow for the love she wishes she had from her mother. Instead, she takes a deep breath, shoving the emotions deeper down in her soul. A second breath shuts the imaginary lid.

"You are such a beautiful girl. I do not understand why you choose to diminish your beauty by dressing the way you do and why you feel like you should act like a male," Sitamun continues. "Do you not see how well your father takes care of our household? Do you not appreciate all that he has given you? Or that I have taught you?"

Red fills the edges of Tiye's vision, fire sealing the box in her heart shut. "Why can't you just let me be who I want to be? Why is me, just as I am, not enough for you?"

"Oh, Tiye, you *are* enough. You have just been led astray from the values we've instilled in you and what Pharaoh Seti proclaims. I blame that boy; he has encouraged you to think you're capable of anything."

"Who I am has nothing to do with Senusret! I am this way because this is who I am. I believe I bring more value to this world than a walking womb or something pretty for someone to look at."

"Tragic, if you honestly believe that," Sitamun answers, her tone infuriatingly mild. "This type of behavior proves my point. You are too irrational to run a household on your own. When you have controlled yourself, come home and we will discuss the marriage options your father has procured."

Sitamun pats Tiye's cheek before walking out of the apothecary. The click of the door snaps the last of Tiye's nerves and she slams her hands down on the workbench, letting out a roar from behind clenched teeth. The movement causes a green tincture to roll off the bench and smash to pieces on the ground.

)) ☾ ((

For the rest of the day, the shop bustles with patrons placing orders or picking them up, keeping Tiye's brain occupied. After the last one leaves with their completed order and she rotates the sign in the window to 'Closed,' Tiye begins mixing up a tincture for her aching joints, when she hears the door creak open.

Rotating to tell Trenko a list of herbs which need to be restocked, she instead finds a male unmistakably not from Ramses standing at the door. Tiye's breath catches, his stature is of someone who is used to being in control. He is dressed in all black; even the scarf covering most of his face to protect against the whipping sands is entirely black.

"I am just finishing up a tincture, but if you let me know what you need, I can get started on it right after this," she says curiously.

Standing stock still, the man stares back at her, not saying a word or moving a muscle.

Emptying her hands and wiping her fingers on her apron, Tiye begins signing to him, repeating what she said out loud. Water lines the man's verdant eyes, and Tiye wonders if the sandstorms are particularly ruthless today. Before she completes signing, Trenko walks in behind the man, moving around to face them both.

"Perfect," he says to the man between them, "you have met the shopkeeper, Tiye. Why are you signing Tiye? Never mind, this is Userkaf, he will be staying in the room above the shop for the time being."

"He is what!?" Tiye spits.

"Watch your tongue, Tiye, your pay will be docked for that insolence. Yes, he will be staying here for at least a week. Isn't that what you said?" Trenko's words are oily as he checks with Userkaf.

"No need to dock her pay; I take no mind. But yes, it will be for at least one week." Userkaf's dark, velvety voice comes out strong despite his mouth still being covered by the scarf.

Transfixed behind the workbench, Tiye scowls at the pair. *Just what I need. The supply trip cannot come soon enough.*

Trenko leads Userkaf to the back of the shop and up the stairs, saying, "I will accept your gold, but you understand it will cost you extra since you don't have our currency. Because of the exchange rate, you see."

Tiye rolls her eyes at the lie slithering smoothly past Trenko's primth-stained teeth.

Tiye scrawls a list of the herbs for Trenko as he returns.

Taking the paper without looking at it, he narrows his eyes at her, speaking quietly, "Do not pull your usual shit with this one, Tiye. I will not lose his money, I am charging him triple. Also, if I find out you've been sleeping on the floor while he is here, I will never rent that room to you."

"I don't know what you're talking about, Trenko, I don't sleep here," Tiye says innocently.

"Sure, sure. You also don't make extra tinctures for yourself without paying, do you? Now make up these for Userkaf, then make yourself scarce."

Tiye moves swiftly, the scent of dried herbs filling the air as she begins with the peculiar tinctures. Unlike her usual tonics to ease pain or cure illnesses, the list calls for combinations of senna, mandrake, and myrrh. *Hopefully, you are not ingesting this, or you are going to simultaneously be constipated and shit your pants while having hallucinations. Not my idea of a good time, but whatever floats your Felucca.*

The shop door clangs shut as Trenko departs, leaving Tiye alone before all the components are even assembled.

CHAPTER NINE

The rest of the week drug on, like vines tethering Tiye to the present moment. Despite her best efforts, she does not see Userkaf again. She's unsure why she even attempts to, but something about the strange male intrigues her. By the end of the week, her misfortune comes to a close. The day of the supply trip is finally here, and in the dark of early morning, Tiye creeps through the silent house with desperately light steps, even using the window in the main room instead of the creaky front door to exit the house. Not even taking a full breath until she's down the street several houses away. Grateful to see no one on her path, Tiye is enveloped in the warmth of the forge as she steps through the entranceway.

"Hey Tiye! You're here early. We don't leave until after sunrise. Do you want to help me finish this dagger for Tawosret?" Senusret asks.

"Sure, how are the defense lessons going with her?" says Tiye.

"She's an exceedingly quick study. I bet she could already hand you your ass."

"Something seems off with that one. But smitten is a good look on you."

They continue forging the dagger in silence until it is tuned to perfection. Starving for fresh air, Tiye steps outside the forge to find dusty pinks and every shade of orange filling the horizon. The sweat dripping down her back freezes in place as the outside air hits it, sending a chill down her spine.

Only after the village begins to stir with life and the sun completes its initial ascent into the sky, does Tiye realize how long she's been watching the horizon. As the last rays burn off the morning chill, she returns to the workshop to find two new people have joined Senusret.

"Tiye, these are the gents we'll be completing the supply run with today," he says. "This is Dryer, and this is Stern. You and I will pull the carts with our camels, while they ride behind us for protection. When we arrive in the city, the three of us will go pick up the supplies as you handle the petition. Once you're finished, you'll meet us back at the supply pickup location. If we have time when you get back, we might look around for information. Don't go sneaking around on your own at any point, got it?"

"Got it."

))☾((

Finding her seat on the rough-hewn bench at the front of the long train of supply carts, Tiye wishes she were with the protection detail on the camels. The sandmar bench offers no comfort, and the lack of fabric to soften the energy jolts has her zapped thighs burning.

Yet, the journey into the Royal City is mercifully short. Senusret stops the cart outside a weathered, single-story stone building where they sit, waiting for a what seems like a baking age as Senusret waits for direction from the male in charge of the warehouse; the battered metal carriage door and flat roof offer little respite from the desert sun.

"Okay, you go get the petition and meet us back right here. The courthouse is only two blocks that way," Senusret says.

"Alright, I'll be right back," Tiye says, jumping from the cart.

"Tiye, I mean it, don't go sneaking around on your own!"

"I won't!" she shouts over her shoulder, as she speeds off.

)) ☽ ((

The sun beats down on the courthouse steps as Tiye emerges, obtained petition in hand, a smile so wide on her face it is painful. The teller's insults are a distant memory as she tucks the precious document carefully into her pocket. With a newfound lightness, Tiye's gaze wanders with a new appreciation for the scenery of the Royal City around her. The vibrant colors of the merchants selling their brightly dyed linens line the streets. Her stomach rumbles as she moves past the wafting smells of enticing foods.

As she nears the warehouse, the calm splinters. Two males bark at each other behind the building, fists shaking in front of them. Pausing, Senusret's warning hovers at the back of her mind, but her feet shift forward. Her gut tells her this isn't something to ignore, but the distance makes it impossible to hear the men's voices.

Feeling the grooves in the stones beneath her hands, Tiye has an idea. Glancing around quickly to ensure no one is watching, she begins to climb the stone wall. It's a quick climb as the warehouse's weathered stones hold many spots with pockets of missing rock, leaving easily accessible handholds.

Her muscles strain as she rolls herself onto the roof. Grit covers her hands as Tiye stays low and then crawls across it.

She positions herself just above the arguing males. One is older, one younger. Both wear loose cream linens marred with dust and grime, Tiye assumes is from their work in the warehouse. Sweat stains run down the armpits and chest of the older man's tunic.

"Khadem, I am sick of having to tell you to do your job! I don't give a shit about your feelings or your laziness. These have to be smashed into the barrels before you add the doum juice. Do not let me find out you've been slacking off again or it will be the rope for you," the older male growls.

"Can you at least tell me what these do? Why does the pharaoh want us to put these in the barrels, Ruman?" Khadem whines.

"It is not for you to question the pharaoh, Khadem, he knows what is best for us. He has brought glory back to our kingdom. Now get back to work."

Peeking over the side, Tiye notices that Khadem is holding a small branch of berries in an unnatural shade of neon yellow in his extended hand. *What in the underworlds are those? And why is Seti putting them in the doum juice?*

With a sunken composure, Khadem follows Ruman back inside the warehouse, shutting the door with a reverberating crash. Maintaining her low position, Tiye crawls to the opposite edge of the building from which she came. Peering over once more, she gracefully rolls herself over the edge, silently dropping the remainder of the distance, then pops up behind a worried-looking Senusret, almost immediately tripping into him.

"So much for a smooth entrance," she mutters.

"What in the underworlds, Tiye? Where have you been and why do you have dust all over you?"

"Don't look so worried, Sen. I'm fine. I'll tell you on the way back."

Closing his eyes momentarily as he shakes his head and

turns his back on her, Senusret propels himself into the cart. Then, he refuses to make eye contact as she hauls herself up into the seat next to him. Tiye sits in silence, feeling the tension radiate off him, breaking it only when they make it well past the perimeter of the Royal City. Senusret's frustration with Tiye's tricks abates only slightly after hearing about what she has seen.

Glancing over his shoulder at the supply carts filled with barrels of doum juice, he says,

"Let's run this by Nakhtmin tonight. They're supposed to be meeting with Nebetah at Pepi's around the time we will get back."

CHAPTER TEN

They are unloading the last of the barrels of doum juice into the storeroom of Pepi's tavern when Nakhtmin and Nebetah walk in. The distrust radiating between the two of them is visible even from Tiye's vantage point at the back of the tavern.

Pepi follows Tiye's line of sight, rolling his eyes. "I'll drain this last one to see if I can find those berries Tiye is talking about," he says. "Hopefully, it's fresh enough that they'll still be reasonably easy to find. I'll bring you whatever I find. You two go on."

Senusret and Tiye leave Pepi to deal with the last barrel, joining the tension-filled table currently occupied by a silent Nakhtmin and Nebetah. Nakhtmin's stern face turns to Senusret as he reclines lazily in his chair. Nebetah looks at Tiye, an eyebrow tugging up as she grins.

Goddess, when she smiles, Tiye muses.

"Alright, I am assuming you are interrupting this meeting

for a reason, tell us what you found." Nakhtmin quips.

"The pharaoh is forcing the warehouse workers to put these bright yellow berries into the doum juice sent out to the kingdom," Tiye answers, noticing an emotion briefly flash across Nebetah's face but is gone before she can understand it.

"Those berries have been a topic of conversation as of late among the guard, but we're unsure what they do or what the pharaoh was doing with them. A small force of the royal guard obtains them from the Cursed Island," Nebetah says in a matter-of-fact tone.

Pepi approaches the table, holding a plate covered with mashed, purple-stained berries. "This is all I could find in the barrel. Can you make anything of this, Tiye?"

Tiye pulls the plate in front of her, closing her eyes, brows knitting together, and hovering her hands just above the contents, concentrating with all her might. "Damn, I can't get anything from them." She rubs the tips of her fingers in circles to ease the building pain in her temples.

"What do you mean you can't get anything from them?" Nebetah asks, cocking her head.

Heat rushes up Tiye's neck as she meets Nebetah's gaze. *Get a hold of yourself,* she thinks. "I-I can read the intentions or spell properties infused in magical plants, but they usually need to be fresh or unused for me to get a reading. These must have been soaking in the doum juice for too long. Maybe if you can tell me how to get out to the island, I … I could get my hands on some fresh berries. Then maybe I can determine their uses."

Again, that flash of emotion Tiye cannot interpret crosses Nebetah's face.

"Yeah, I can help if we head out tonight. It might take a few hours to get there, but we need a boat to get us out to the island," Nebetah says.

"I have a small rowboat I used to fish the pond before it dried up. You can use that," Pepi offers.

"Perfect and I am free tomorrow too. No one will miss me. Let's do it!" Tiye almost yells.

She ignores the fear that bubbles up at the thought of venturing to the famed island. She has heard stories for years of the monsters that roam its sands, corrupted from the curse of Isis. It is claimed Isis, angered by destruction the inhabitants were causing to her beloved world, cursed the island and the animals, giving them powers to destroy any who trespassed there.

"Tiye, the island is cursed! It is called Cursed Island for a reason! I get that you're reckless, but maybe there's another way?" Senusret exclaims.

"And do what, Sen? March into the castle and nicely ask the pharaoh or his special guard to hand over the berries for me to examine?" Tiye retorts.

Senusret groans, his eyes squeezing shut as his head falls back to face the ceiling.

"Unfortunately, I agree with them, Senusret. We can't exactly warn the people of the village or even those still with the rebellion until we know what we are dealing with. They would die of dehydration without the doum juice. Time is not on our side here," Nakhtmin says.

Nebetah's eyes seem to pierce each one of them in the room, holding them steady with her serious, violet gaze. Then Senusret, realizing he is outnumbered, throws his hands up in defeat.

))☽((

Within two hours, Tiye and Nebetah saddle two camels that will take them to the shore, pulling Pepi's small rowboat behind them in one of the empty supply carts. But before they can take off, Pepi pulls Tiye to the side.

"Tiye, I don't like that you're going with her alone. I don't trust her, and neither does Nakhtmin; I can tell," he hisses urgently.

Although both Nakhtmin and Pepi are private by nature, it has not eluded Tiye that they've developed a romantic entanglement over the last several years.

"Why can't this wait until at least Senusret can go with you too?" Pepi pleads.

"Pepi, you worry too much," Tiye says, placing her hand on Pepi's arm. "Sen has work tomorrow and Nebetah and I already have the day off. It is perfect timing. Nebetah won't be off duty for another week, and she knows where the island is. We know the pharaoh's guard goes there regularly. So it can't be that dangerous."

Senusret saunters up, agreeing for once, "Yeah, Pepi, if she doesn't go tonight, she won't be able to spend alone time with her new crush."

"Oh, shut up, you two. Quit worrying." Tiye walks away, swinging herself onto the camel. She leans over the camel's neck, giving the animal a loving pat. Sitting back up, Tiye secures her scarf around her hair and face, leaving only her eyes visible. Looking to her right, she sees that Nebetah has done the same. Tiye is grateful for the scarf in this moment, feeling a blush rise up her neck to her cheeks as she catches Nebetah's eyes looking her up and down.

"If you two are done ogling one another, shouldn't you get going? I thought we were in a hurry and all," Senusret snarks.

Groaning, Tiye nudges her camel forward. "See you tomorrow night." Then, easing her camel into a trot, she catches up to Nebetah with the rowboat in tow, and they set out into the wide expanse of dunes before them.

CHAPTER ELEVEN

The endless landscape of sand holds Tiye captive as she rides silently behind Nebetah. After several hours of hard riding, the coastline comes into view on the horizon, even though it's still at least another hour away. The sun starts to set soon after they first spot it and, as the cold begins to penetrate Tiye's sore muscles, she starts to wonder how she will manage a conversation with Nebetah now that they're on their own. Tiye's social woes plague her mind for the remainder of the journey before Nebetah halts her camel with quite some distance left to the shoreline.

"We will camp here for the night," she states.

"You don't want to move closer to the shoreline? Wouldn't it be harder for us to be spotted if we were closer?" Tiye asks, unsure.

"This should be fine. I am sure no one will see us from here."

It seems more exposed where they are but Tiye has never

been to the shore before, she'll have to take Nebetah's word for it.

They busy themselves unpacking their bedrolls, adding netting to keep out the glivners. Tiye hands Nebetah some dried meat and a paratha, and their fingers graze, sending a tingling sensation up Tiye's arm. *Breathe, just breathe,* she reminds herself. Her eyes raise to meet Nebetah's, whose lavender orbs are fixed on her face with the same appraising expression as when they started their ride this afternoon.

In the next moment, the camels began spitting at each other, disrupting the moment.

Tiye nestles herself on the bedroll, conforming the sand underneath to shape to her body as she chews on her own ration of dried meat. Wishing her brain had more to say than provide snarky commentary, she sits in silence pulling apart her paratha.

Nebetah speaks first, "So, what was it like growing up in Ramses?"

"It was alright." Tiye shrugs. "I mean I'm sure it was just as boring as any of the other villages of Famsastu. And just as backwards. What was it like growing up in the Royal City?"

"My parents and I were extraordinarily fortunate that Pharaoh Seti not only did not execute us for being part of the fallen pharaoh's empire, but also for allowing us to keep our home and for my father to remain with the guard. It took a long time for the new guard and their families to stop treating us and the few other families poorly. It got better until I became the first female in Pharaoh Seti's guard, which has brought a lot of the poor treatment back." A pained expression creases Nebetah's face as she speaks.

"It sounds like a pretty lonely place to be. Are your parents supportive?"

"Yes, they're wonderful. We'd better get some rest for tomorrow," Nebetah says abruptly.

Finishing the last of her paratha, Nebetah rolls onto her side, facing away from Tiye who mimics the action, rolling with her back to Nebetah, ensuring her netting is secured.

Damn what did I say? Did I upset her?

But even the questions whirling in Tiye's head do not stop the sleep coming, and she rolls over her as soon as she shuts her eyes, exhaustion of the day taking its toll.

CHAPTER TWELVE

Sounds of the water crashing into the shore fills Tiye's ears as the light of the rising sun forces her awake. Kaleidoscope colors ripple in every direction as she takes in the water for the first time. The sight makes her life feel so small in comparison, bringing with it the knowledge of how little of the world she has seen. The sun, nestled among the vibrant colors, illuminates the island, its seemingly calm landscape contrary to its given name: the Cursed Island.

Turning to find Nebetah's bedroll vacant, Tiye scrambles off her own. Her heart hammers as she looks around in every direction, her brain calculating the best options as to how to find Nebetah. Before any ideas solidify into action, Nebetah makes her appearance over a mound of sand in the direction they came from yesterday, shoving her hands into her pocket as she does.

Collecting herself, Tiye hopes Nebetah cannot see her panicked state from the distance. Her breaths even out as

Nebetah makes it back to their camp site. "Good morning, did you sleep well?" she asks.

"I did, how about you?" Nebetah says cheerfully.

"Same. Do you want breakfast before we head to the island?" Tiye passes Nebetah dried figs and a paratha.

They eat quickly in silence, then make quick work of packing up the campsite back onto the backs of the camels. Using the animals to pull the cart, they tow the rowboat to the water's edge where Nebetah guides it into the water. She instructs Tiye with calm soothing tones, leaving only the stern submerged in the water so as not to damage the rudder, nor let the craft float away on its own. With the boat secured in place, they lead the camels and the cart back away from the shoreline. They bury the neck of the cart in the sand, then use the cart as an anchor, tying the leads of their camels to the cart and thus preventing them from running off.

"Are you ready for this?" Nebetah asks as they approach the rowboat once more.

"Ready as I'll ever be," answers Tiye.

"You hop in first and I will push us off."

Hands clutched on either side of the bow, Tiye stretches her leg out before her as far as she can, leaving her other foot securely in the sand. Tapping her foot along the bottom of the boat, finding a solid placement, she eases herself over the edge. Tiye's heart stutters as the transport rocks from side to side.

"Here's to hoping I don't have to learn how to swim today." She laughs nervously, more to steady herself than anything.

Tiye finds a seat in the center of the transom and, seeing this, Nebetah pushes the boat further into the water, jumping at the last moment as the bow loses purchase with the sand. She lands elegantly on the hull, like a cat, rocking the boat only slightly, and her face lights up with a genuine smile when she looks at Tiye. Dread eases from Tiye's muscles as she basks in this. Nebetah guides Tiye over to one side of the thwart to make room for herself on the small transom. The size of it forces them to sit with their thighs grazing each other, bringing a new kind of tension back to Tiye.

Nebetah meets Tiye's face again with a comforting smile. "Let me get us facing the right direction and then we can row together. Here, this is how you hold your oar out of the water. Hold it like this while I get us positioned."

Nebetah's hand covers Tiye's which is wrapped around the oar, pushing it down to meet Tiye's thigh, propelling the larger end out of the water. Nebetah turns, pulling the rudder to her while stroking her oar, propelling the stern away from the security of the land and towards the island.

"Now, drop your oar into the water and I will show you how to complete a stroke," she says.

She laces her fingers over Tiye's, holding the oar gently, and guiding her arm to complete the same stroking mechanism. Tiye observes Nebetah reposition the boat, the rhythmic splash of water against the hull filling the air, mesmerized.

"The key is to stroke the oars in sync. Now you try." Nebetah's fingers slide away from Tiye's hand, slowly working their way down to rest by her elbow.

Entrenched in making sure her strokes are timed with Nebetah's, Tiye does not notice the lingering touch until it is gone.

It doesn't take long for action to feel natural, moving them across the water with surprising speed. They make it more than halfway to the island before a dark shadow looms towards the rowboat. Instantly, Nebetah pushes both oars down, thrusting them out of the water. Seeing the color drain from Nebetah's face stops Tiye from asking what the matter is.

As it seems to move below them, Tiye can see the shadow is at least three times the size of the boat. She watches aghast as it appears just on the other side, an alarming tail covered in teal scales. It shoots out of the water, ending in eight spikes, only to slither back under the surface seconds after its initial appearance. Both women sit frozen in place for a long while, staring in the direction of the disappearing shadow.

Tiye breaks the silence whispering, despite the distance, "What the fuck was that?"

"That is the Ammit, Devourer of Souls. Pray to the gods we do not meet them again on this journey." Nebetah wipes sweat from her brow, color slowly returning to her face.

Fueled by the adrenaline coursing through their veins after their narrow escape, they close the remainder of the distance to the island's shoreline quickly.

Tiye assured Pepi and Senusret that she didn't truly believe the island was cursed, but doubts inch their way into her mind. What if her hasty decisions put her and Nebetah in real danger? *If it has to be anyone, at least it is me. Hopefully I just don't take Nebetah with me if I die.*

As the shoreline draws closer, Nebetah instructs Tiye once more, increasing their speed to run the boat aground. Not waiting for the rowboat to quit moving, Nebetah leaps over the bow onto the sand, pulling the boat further onto the bank and making it easier for Tiye to navigate her way out. Together, they free the boat from the water and finally turn to take in the view of Cursed Island.

CHAPTER THIRTEEN

Just beyond the sandy shoreline, the island seems to consist entirely of the largest boulders Tiye has ever seen. Each one varies in size and texture, but all are composed of a black, iridescent rock, creating a solid wall blocking the interior of the island from view. The initial view of the reflective light bouncing off the water hitting the shiny stone, sends goosebumps up Tiye's arms. Shaking off the chill, she takes in the sight of the rock face once more. "Where do you think we should start trying to climb?" She beams at Nebetah with the prospect of this once-in-a-lifetime opportunity.

Nebetah's eyebrows slam together as her jaw goes slack, mouth opening slightly, the horror evident on her face at the suggestion. "First, let's check for any breaks in the boulders before we start risking our necks. You check that way, and I'll look this way. Go three hundred paces and then come back if you don't find anything before that."

Shoulder slumping in disappointment, Tiye slowly makes

her way in the direction Nebetah indicated. She searches around every boulder within the designated perimeter. Not finding anything that resembles a path after reaching her three hundredth step, she trudges back to the starting point.

Making it back to the original position first, Tiye starts testing out the available handholds, making it about halfway up the rock face with relative ease. Her long athletic form has been a source of teasing for the boys throughout her childhood, but Tiye always appreciated her height and the strength that comes naturally to her.

She spots Nebetah marching back in her direction. Silently, she drops the rest of the way down, joy overwhelming her chest as her knees hit the sand. "Did you have any luck finding a path?" she asks.

"Yeah, about a hundred paces or so that way, there is a break in the boulders with a trail that seems to head to the center of the island," Nebetah says.

Tiye notices Nebetah's shirt is rumpled from sleep and clinging to her chest. Her usually neat straight hair that has come loose from her plait is plastered to her head from the heat and sweat, as it sticks up in multiple directions.

Retracing Nebetah's steps, they come to the break in the boulders that is strategically concealing the path from view from anyone who might be on the water or the mainland. The perfection of the path's entrance appears to be simultaneously a natural formation, and a manufactured one. Boulders flanking the path on either side grow taller the further they walk, while the trail gently inclines.

The pathway is wide enough for them to walk side by side, seeing nothing else but the stunning rock face and the open trail ahead. The sun continues its movement into the sky as they continue this way for over an hour. Sweat drips down Tiye's back as they reach a fork in the path.

"Should we take this one?" Nebetah asks, pointing to the

path to the left.

Quickly glancing down both paths, which look nearly identical, Tiye takes a drink from her waterskin, finding it close to half full. *Am I hearing that right? She's asking me?* She contemplates for a moment longer before deciding on the path to the right. "Let's take this one. I think it will be worth it," Tiye says.

Nebetah chews on her lower lip before starting her way down it, closing the distance between them. "Fine."

After a few minutes, a strange rushing sound can be heard and Tiye picks up her pace, confident she has made the right choice.

"Tiye, I think we should turn back, try the other path?" Nebetah says.

"Trust me, for just a little bit longer. Even if it doesn't get us to what we are looking for, I bet it will be worth it."

Hesitating momentarily, Nebetah increases her pace to match Tiye's as they continue. After a few more minutes where Tiye worries her ears were playing tricks on her, a bend in the path opens to a spectacular aquamarine body of water encapsulated by the same obsidian rock. A thin rushing waterfall crashes down into the water below, opposite where they stand, churning white and sending up sheets of spray. The rushing sound is now a deafening roar. Past the opening, a crescent of sand lines the edge of the water. With tentative movements, Nebetah stops in place just beyond the opening. Goosebumps run up Tiye's arm as she glides her hands through the water, the temperature cooling her overheated flesh. Cupping water in both hands, Tiye takes a sip, testing it. It's wonderful and she refills her waterskin, replacing the usual doum juice.

Using a large rock at the water's edge as a seat, Tiye begins stripping down to her undergarments. After removing her boots, she peels the sweat-soaked clothing away from her body and lies it out to dry in the sun. All the while, Nebetah hasn't moved, now stumbling forward as Tiye steps into the water.

"What are you doing? You don't know what is in that water!" she almost shrieks.

"Oh, come on in, don't be scared. It feels great! You can keep your clothes on if that makes you feel more comfortable," Tiye retorts. The goosebumps now cover her body as she waits for a response. "At least refill your waterskin if you won't get in."

"Tiye, get out of there right now!" Nebetah shouts, scowling as she crosses her arms under her chest in a tight knot.

Tiye continues walking until the water reaches above her waist. Submerging beneath the surface, she feels her sand-chapped skin cool instantly. She takes a few moments with only the sound of the plunging waterfall underwater pummeling her senses, her body feels weightless. The sensation is heavenly but it doesn't last. Sneaking a triumphant look at Nebetah as she breaks the surface of the water, she sees Nebetah perched close, staring at something with apprehension.

For a single moment, Tiye can't process.

Nebetah gapes at the sand covering her feet, now past her ankles.

In a flash, Tiye's heart sinks into her stomach as she registers the whole sight. Without a second thought, she scrambles out of the water. "Nebetah, your feet!" she calls out at the top of her voice, clambering onto the rock where she discarded her clothes. Swiftly, she ties her tunic to her breeches, testing the knot's strength. "Here, grab the end of this!"

The sand now reaches almost halfway to Nebetah's knees as she catches the end of Tiye's makeshift rope, her panicked cries competing with the waterfall in the idyllic alcove. Tiye pulls with all her strength, using the rock as leverage, but Nebetah just sinks further into the quicksand, her head frantically whipping this way and that, eyes bulging.

"Nebetah, I need you to trust me. Can you do that?" Tiye calls.

"Yes anything, please just get me out of here!"

"Okay. Take off your tunic and tie it to the end of the rope. Loop it around you," she says.

They have switched positions and now it is Tiye instructing Nebetah. The other woman hastily removes her tunic, tying and securing it as she is told.

"Perfect, now thread the loop around both of your arms. Once you have a tight hold, I need you to lie on the sand so you can use the leverage to push your legs free. As soon as they're clear, roll onto your stomach and I will pull you away and over to this rock."

"You're insane! You want me to lie down on this death sand!" Nebetah shrieks.

"Nebetah, please trust me! We have to do this quickly before the quicksand is above your knees!" *If she doesn't listen, she'll slip under the sand faster than I can help,* Tiye thinks.

Tears streaming down her face, Nebetah secures her arms in the improvised loop, her whole-body quaking as she lies down on the sand. Straining to push her legs free, the seconds pass like blades slicing her skin. Nebetah's jaw is clenched so hard the tendons in her neck stand out.

The sand does not move an inch.

Tiye pulls furiously, her arms locked and straining, breath coming in gasps as the muscles in her stomach clench. *I won't be left on this island alone!* But it's too hard, too unyielding. Nothing is happening. She is about to slacken her hold, just to catch her breath, when she feels movement. Suddenly, as Tiye pulls, the sand around Nebetah's knees begins to quake in unnaturally smooth waves. She doesn't let go and the sand crests open reluctantly, freeing its hostage hold on Nebetah's legs. As Tiye feels the give, she yells at Nebetah, "Roll!"

Nebetah does not waste a moment to roll to her front, after which, Tiye pulls with all her might, inching Nebetah along the sand to the rock edge she has positioned herself on top of. Her hands within reach, Tiye drops the fabric, helping Nebetah onto the rock.

Scrambling up next to Tiye, Nebetah wraps her in a bone-crushing embrace, her shaking slowly beginning to subside.

With her face still close to Tiye's, Nebetah wipes her tears as she states, "Thank you so much for saving me!"

"Of course, we couldn't have the rebellion lose their best spy," Tiye chuckles lightly.

With her face so close to Nebetah's, Tiye can see the tracks Nebetah's tears have made through the dust clinging to her cheeks, and she realizes there are three shades of violet that make up the color of her eyes. Tiye's gaze lands on Nebetah's supple, full lips as they slightly part, releasing a light gasp, causing heat to pool low in her abdomen. Her eyes slam back up, meeting the greedy look Nebetah is giving her.

Tiye slowly leans in. *What in the underworlds is going on here*, she thinks to herself. *Would it be ridiculous to think that Nebetah might be … interested in me?*

CHAPTER FOURTEEN

Nebetah jerks back with a screech. Putting distance between them, she jabs her finger at Tiye's shoulder. Without the distraction of the other woman so close, Tiye notices a foreign weight present on her left shoulder. As she goes to grab the object, it scurries down her left arm to stop on her palm. Tiye's shock subsides as she takes in a brightly colored slender creature, about the length of her hand. The creature has the shape of a salamander, its scaly skin ranging from neon pink to bright orange. However, its most peculiar feature is the dragonfly-like wings that protrude just behind the shoulder joints on its front legs. The shimmering translucent wings lie flat against the creature's back as it sits in her palm, mouth cracked into what can only be described as a smile with its tail waggling off the edge of her hand.

"Well, aren't you adorable!" Tiye stares at the little ... guy. It's as if she can feel what is going on in his little head, as if *he* has been with her all of her life. *I don't know why, and how I know he is a he, but he just feels like he's mine,* Tiye thinks.

"Put that down; it could be poisonous!" Nebetah's voice is coarse, scratchy after the sand ordeal.

"Oh, I am sure he won't bite me, right?" Tiye continues looking at the rainbow creature, resisting the urge to pet him.

"Well, at least get dressed. We need to get a move on." Nebetah seems to struggle with finding a semblance of order, or instruction as she unties the knotted clothes.

Huffing as she pulls her tunic back over her head, she then extends Tiye's clothes out to her.

Setting the creature carefully down on the rock, Tiye, suddenly self-conscious, takes her disentangled clothes from Nebetah, turning to face away as she pulls them back into place. Once fully clothed again, she refills Nebetah's waterskin from the lake and together, they exit the rock, cautiously avoiding the quicksand by jumping on patches of grass or mossy boulders. Wary of staying still in one location for too long, they set off back up the path. As they do, finally leaving the alcove behind them, the foreign weight returns to her shoulder and Tiye looks down to see the creature has perched itself on her shoulder again.

A soft smile breaks across her face as he finds his spot, and she can't help but feel at home. "Alright, you can come with us for the time being. But first, we shall give you a name, eh?" Nebetah groans from Tiye's other side. "I've got it, Ahmose! With wings like the moon, you surely are a child of Isis."

Ahmose nuzzles appreciatively against the underside of her chin, then curls up on her shoulder. The walk back to the fork in the path seemed to take no time at all. The onyx boulders continue along the new path, the same as the other paths. However, here, the further they walk, it seems that the boulders steadily decrease in size as their route continues to incline.

After walking for about half an hour, the path opens into a

field that stretches as far as Tiye can see. It is filled with dark green bushes overflowing with matching-colored leaves, each bearing yellow berries at various stages of ripeness. At the center of the field is a magnificent limestone pyramid, the size of a courthouse; it seems so out of place with all the dark green plants surrounding it.

"Huh," Tiye grunts. "I wonder what's in there?"

"We don't have time to explore that. Can you just figure out what these plants do so we can get out of here?" Nebetah doesn't bother to hide her irritation.

"Oh, I am sure we can take a quick look around. It will only take a minute."

"Tiye, your last reckless decision almost got me killed. We came here to check out these plants; let's do that and get back. Plus, I have duty in the morning that I cannot be late for."

Tiye's face flushes as she tries to see things from Nebetah's perspective. "Right, of course. Sorry about the whole almost getting you killed thing ..." Head low, she walks over to the closest bush with ripe berries. Sinking down to her knees next to the plant, she finds a cluster to concentrate on. "Alright, let's see what these can do." She lifts her hand, letting the bundle rest in her palm, and slowly closes her eyes. The familiar feeling of warmth spreads up her arm, cascading across her chest. Her magic swirls within her, untangling the intentions within the berries. "It seems the berries have two intentions," she says after some minutes have passed. "They either suppress magic, not too much, just slightly dampen it, but they significantly affect healing magic. Or, they have nutritional properties of some kind for magical beings." Tiye frowns as she holds the small yellow bunch in her hand.

"Hmm. I don't know what that means, but I'm inclined to be suspicious," Nebetah offers, her irate tone softened.

"There's no way to know why the pharaoh is putting the

berries in the doum juice," Tiye muses. Opening her eyes, she sees relief wash over Nebetah's face.

Ahmose, who has crawled down her arm, his tongue shooting out to latch around and snatch a berry, quickly swallows it, afterward immediately running back up her arm to find his place on her shoulder. *Why would Seti be putting these in the doum juice? What does he gain from it?*

"Great," Nebetah sighs, "Now that we know what it does, let's please just get out of here."

Turning back to view the pyramid again, a twinge pinches Tiye's gut, and then a hand slides into hers, befuddling the feeling. She looks back to discover an expression of pure joy on Nebetah's face.

"It was so incredible to watch your magic work," Nebetah says, changed. She gives Tiye's hand a little squeeze. "Let's go home."

With Nebetah's hand still holding hers, they return to the path. After a while, her hand slips from Tiye's as they establish a steady pace for the return trip to the shore.

Their steady movement knocks loose a question from Tiye's mind. "You know, I don't actually know what your magic is, Nebetah," she says.

"Oh, I'm a healer. It's not exactly a strong selling point for being in the guard, but it's useful when someone gets injured on duty. And clearly, the berries aren't affecting me enough to hinder my healing abilities. So that's good news."

"I bet that is extremely helpful as a guard. I am sorry it sounds like it isn't appreciated," Tiye answers thoughtfully.

A comfortable silence settles over the remainder of the hike, which is mostly uneventful, save for the curses Tiye mutters under her breath as she stumbles on multiple occasions. She is grateful Ahmose appears to possess great grip strength. Despite all her wobbling, the little creature remains steady on her shoulder through every misstep, nuzzling her each time she regains her balance. His steady presence has become a quick comfort.

As they crest the opening of the pathway to the shoreline, they discover their fortune has steadily increased since the incident with the quicksand as the rowboat remains in the same spot they left it in when they began their exploration this morning. Together, Tiye and Nebetah set about moving it back into the water, replicating its position from earlier in the day.

"Nebetah, do you think I could have a minute with Ahmose before we leave?" Tiye asks.

Nebetah dips her head in acknowledgment while standing by the boat as Tiye tenderly picks Ahmose up from her shoulder, positioning him on her palm in front of her face.

"Hey buddy, I'm sorry, but I have to leave you here, okay? It's not safe for you where I'm going. But know that I'm going to miss you a lot." Tiye gently sets Ahmose down on the sand but he immediately attempts to crawl back onto her. Holding him back, Tiye pleads, "I'm really sorry, Ahmose, but you have to stay here."

With that, Ahmose plops his hindquarters down on the sand, hanging his head. Tiye slowly walks over to the rowboat and carefully climbs in. As she positions herself on the transom once more, she waves to Ahmose, who is sitting on the beach just a few feet away, staring pitifully back at her, before looking away.

Nebetah pushes the rowboat out into the water fully, jumping in as gracefully as she did earlier, only this time, when her face meets Tiye's, it seems to be questioning if she is okay. Moving into position next to Tiye, Nebetah's leg gently nudges hers, though it does not have the full effect on Tiye as it did before. Mercifully, on their journey back across the water to the mainland, they do not encounter the Ammit again.

)) ☾ ((

The camels are spitting at each other once more as Tiye and Nebetah pull the rowboat up out of the water on the mainland. Digging out the tongue of the cart takes no time at all because at least half of the sand they placed on top of it has been shifted by the wind while they were away. Attaching the cart to the camels, Tiye and Nebetah secure the rowboat back into place.

"Maybe we should eat," Tiye says as her stomach grumbles, partially from hunger, and partially in anticipation of being next to Nebetah for the long journey ahead.

They make quick work of devouring their stores of parathas and dried meat before setting off into the endless sand.

Tiye's thoughts begin to wander within minutes, the unending landscape of sand touching wide all around her. Something gnaws at her gut, but whatever it is keeps floating just out of reach. The frustration begins to mount as the thought evades her capture when Nebetah's hand extends to grip Tiye's shoulder.

"I can tell that was hard for you to leave Ahmose, but it was the right thing to do," she says.

"It was. Thanks for saying so, though." It seems odd to Tiye that she forged a connection to the creature so quickly. Realizing belatedly she should not have named him, she internally chides herself. Nebetah's hand slides down Tiye's arm, clasping her hand and giving it a squeeze. As she slowly slides her fingers away, leaning fully onto her own camel again, Tiye's stomach fills with butterflies in a way she's never felt before.

Hours pass without another word. The silence trails on when a small piercing feeling hits her ear, causing Tiye to swear loudly. Feeling the ear in question, Tiye finds what is quickly becoming a familiar weight and the corresponding nuzzling under her chin. Strategically, she removes Ahmose from her shoulder, turning her body to hide him from Nebetah's view.

"How did you get here?" she whispers from the side of her mouth. "Never mind, just don't let Nebetah see you. She thinks you're back on the island." Tiye smiles despite herself and twists her arm to place her hand where Ahmose rests on her lower back.

"Are you alright?" Nebetah asks.

"Yep, it must have been a spider or something. It's gone now." A smile tugs at her lips as she feels Ahmose run up her back to burrow under her scarf, which hangs loosely around her neck and head. There he remains for the rest of the journey.

CHAPTER FIFTEEN

Upon their return to the village, they head straight to the tavern, where they are greeted by Pepi, who helps them unload the camels. As the sun begins its descent below the horizon, Senusret and Tawosret stride toward the tavern. Tawosret's neck and face are flushed as she looks away from Senusret, her eyes finding Tiye and Nebetah.

Senusret rushes over to hug Tiye, picking her up as he does. "Hey, you made it back! So, she didn't get you killed after all?"

"Excuse me!" Nebetah throws her hands onto her hips, "I did not almost get her killed; she, on the other hand, almost got *me* killed. And who are you again?"

"But I also saved you after," Tiye interjects, "not that you're bitter about it at all. Put me down, Sen."

"You almost died?" Tawosret squeaks in Nebetah's direction.

At the same time, Senusret groans, head rolling back as if

he is praying to the gods above for patience. "Of course you did."

"It's fine, we are back now. Tawosret, can I have a word with you for a moment?" Nebetah asks, leading Tawosret a few steps away.

Tiye and Senusret watch the two during their brief exchange. They could not look more different. Tawosret is stunning in a pale pink dress that hugs her curves, her dark braids pinned back neatly out of her face. Whereas Nebetah's once cream tunic and pants are covered in grime and sand. More hair has come loose from her braid, flying in every direction.

"I have to get back to the Royal City." Nebetah says, and subtly grabs Tiye's hand, giving it a swift squeeze before letting go.

Her proximity and touch send a blaze through Tiye. "Of course, I will let everyone know what we found," Tiye says, her tongue thick.

"Thanks. I'm sure I'll see you soon." Nebetah walks away smoothly, mounting her camel, and heading off in the direction of the Royal City.

Within minutes, she is a speck in the distance. As the final rays of sunlight dip below the sand, the trio enters the tavern, each finding a seat at a table near the bar. With the tavern empty, Pepi makes his way around the bar to join them at the table.

"Did you really almost get Nebetah killed?" Tawosret inquires, horror tightening her face.

"Well, sorta." Tiye shrugs as she pushes her scarf from the top of her, fabric landing loosely around her shoulders with the rest.

Senusret practically dumps his chair over as he scrambles away from where Tiye sits, with Ahmose now exposed on her shoulder. "What in the name of Goddess is that thing?"

Cackling with laughter, Tiye sets Ahmose on the table in front of her. Her laughter subsiding, she introduces him, "This is Ahmose. He is such a sweet boy! He found us on the island and did not want to stay, apparently. He snuck his way onto the boat on our return trip across the water."

Senusret repositions himself back in his chair at the table, cautiously leaning forward to observe Tawosret as she coos over Ahmose stroking the top of his head with a finger. Tiye tells the group about her trip. From crossing the water with the terrifying Ammit to the island's obsidian boulders, to the outlandish pathway. She explains how Nebetah became trapped in the quicksand and how Ahmose found them. Finally, she tells of how the second pathway led them to a field with an unexpected pyramid and what she uncovered about the intentions of the berries.

"You mean to tell me that the pharaoh is either intentionally suppressing all magical beings' powers or simply adding extra nutrients?" Senusret asks incredulously. "I find it very hard to believe that evil git doesn't know anything about the additional nutrients. Do either of you think you can counteract what the berries are doing to the doum juice?" He looks back and forth between Pepi and Tiye.

"I can work on it at the apothecary now that I know what I am working with. That is, if you can spare some of the doum juice for me to work with, Pepi?" Tiye asks.

"I'll set some aside for you. Once you have a way to counteract the berries, I can work on replicating it for all the barrels," Pepi says.

Tiye nods, the smell of stale mead and primth smoke lingering in the air. *I hope this works. I don't know what Seti is doing to us, but it can't be good.*

"Now that that's settled, tell us about this pyramid. Was it the pharaoh's crazy sex dungeon or what?"

"Gross, Sen, I didn't want those images in my head. No, I

don't know what was in it. We didn't go in."

"Seriously? You're telling me, with your unending curiosity and risk-taking, *you* didn't go in. Why in the underworlds not?" he pushes.

"Nebetah was still a little freaked out by my almost getting her killed in the quicksand. She didn't want to test our luck anymore by checking it out."

Tawosret, who has remained silent the whole time, finally speaks, "I think it's unfair of Nebetah to blame you for the quicksand; it seems like an accident. You didn't do it on purpose, and it sounds like your fast thinking saved her life."

"Thank you, but I can understand how she was feeling. I was being reckless getting into the water when we knew we still hadn't found what we were looking for, especially not knowing anything about the area," Tiye demurs.

Tawosret's empty glass clinks as she sets it down on the table.

"Still, recklessness aside, you don't find it odd she didn't want to explore the pyramid?" Senusret counters, siding with Tawosret.

"No, Sen, I don't. She seemed really freaked out." Tiye answers.

"Alright, I'll drop it," he says, putting his palms up, then leans forward, "But … we still have the boat, and you know the way now. We could go back next week to check out what Seti is hiding in that thing?" He waits for her answer with his handsome, infectious grin.

Tiye considers this. It doesn't take long. She *does* want to know what is in the pyramid, and it would be a fast trip. *What could go wrong?*

"Okay, but you have to promise me you won't tell Nebetah either about this, *or* Ahmose. She thinks he is still back on the Island. And she already thinks I am reckless enough," Tiye says, grinning despite herself.

"Even better!" Senusret says. "Everyone promise not to tell anyone outside the four of us at this table."

CHAPTER SIXTEEN

Three weeks pass without an opportunity for Tiye and Senusret to take a trip out to the island. While they wait, Tiye settles into her quaint new living quarters above the apothecary, where she is only subjected to two enraged outbursts on separate occasions from her mother about the disgrace she has become and the dishonor she is bringing to their family. Userkaf moved out.

One of these spats is conducted without her mother realizing that Trenko is standing in the room until it is too late. However, Tiye suspects her mother doesn't much care as she shoots him a scathing look upon exiting the shop—as if he is to blame for 'the predicament' her daughter finds herself in. As a result, Trenko is kinder to Tiye following this interaction, though only slightly.

Following these visits, Teti comes to see her at the shop, something he has never done before, in an attempt to get her to move back to their parent's house. Tiye vehemently rejects the request. So, she is not surprised when she asks him, and Teti adamantly refuses, to help her grab the rest of her limited belongings that still remain at their parents' house. Nice.

However, these unfortunate interactions cannot dampen Tiye's excitement of finally having some control over her life. She doesn't have much to fill the small space, but she has never felt more at home. In addition to the freedom she feels, Ahmose has become her constant companion, bringing life to her residence as he scampers or increasingly flies about.

The first time he flies in front of Tiye, it seems he is just as shocked as she is to see himself hovering in the air. She has worried about what he would eat, but he quickly takes to consuming the small beetles and other insects flying or scuttling around the apothecary. Tiye has come to the realization that she will have to tell Nebetah about Ahmose, as it seems unlikely he will return there. But she will deal with that problem another day. As if understanding his uniqueness here and the possible threat it presents, Ahmose instantly hides whenever anyone other than Senusret or Tawosret comes around.

Nakhtmin decides, with Pepi, Senusret, Tiye and Tawosret, that it is in the best interests of the village not to inform anyone else in the rebellion about the berries in the doum juice until a remedy is found, as the fear might outweigh the reality that the villagers do not have enough water to survive. Furthermore, as Tawosret is now spending significant amounts of time in the pharaoh's healers' presence, Nakhtmin is determined that in addition to combat training she was doing with Senusret, she will now complete magic training with Tiye.

As the only other witch in the group, Tiye will train Tawosret in the ways of magic. There is a chance she will need to dampen it so as not to raise suspicions when Tiye comes up with a fix for the doum juice.

In the smaller villages witches are generally left to their own devices to train themselves with magic. Pharaoh Seti refused to pay for the traveling Magi group when he came into power, claiming it is the responsibility of the villages to train their people the way they see fit. The door of the apothecary creaks open as Tiye curses the sample of doum juice taunting her. Completing twenty-two attempts so far to no avail, it mocks her in its jar, unchanged.

"Oh no, what is wrong? Are you okay?" Tawosret asks.

"Yeah, it is just that this goddess-damned doum juice will not give in," Tiye huffs, throwing a long-handled spoon on her work bench. After giving the doum juice one last quick death stare, she turns to face Tawosret. Her curly brown hair is intricately woven into numerous long plaits, delicately fashioned into a crown atop her head, and her dark skin contrasts beautifully with her cream-colored kalasiris. Beholding her beauty, Tiye truly understands why Senusret is so taken with the healer and wonders if Tawosret could be the one to end his philandering ways, though she does not voice this, of course.

"But that is not why you are here. Today we are going to start off by understanding your magic." Tiye wipes her hands on her apron and then removes it, folding it over the back of a chair. She pokes about with her hair, twisting any stray strands away from her face, and gestures Tawosret toward a cleared space on a large table for them both to sit. "Did you get a chance to train your magic at all with the traveling Magi?"

"No," Tawosret says, a frown in her voice.

"No problem. Do you know what your magic requires for you to use it? For instance, with my magic when I use it, I am drained of energy the longer I do it. What happens with yours?" Tiye asks.

"I don't know. I have never noticed anything," Tawosret

answers.

Tiye grimaces for a moment, then pulls the dagger from the sheath she now wears on her thigh. Rapidly, she lays the dagger on her palm, slashing across it, and leaving a trail of blood in its wake as a hiss passes her lips.

"Oh, my Goddess, what have you done?" Tawosret lunges forward, but before she can reach her, Tiye pulls her hand out of reach, holding the other out in front to stop Tawosret's movement.

"Obviously, I want you to heal this, but when you do, I want you to pay attention to the energy of the magic and how it flows through your body," she says calmly.

Tawosret tentatively reaches forward again, hovering her delicate hands over Tiye's bleeding one, and Tiye watches as her magic slowly stitches the wound back together, a warmth starting in her chest and moving down to the slashed skin, leaving a wake of chill behind. The cut on her hand seals as if it never existed, the only tell-tale evidence, crusted blood caked around the nonexistent wound.

"Did you feel anything?" she asks. *Woo, I am tired. I must have overdone it with the doum juice.*

The corners of Tawosret's lip turned down as she responds, "No, nothing."

"You didn't notice *any* drain of your energy?" Tiye asks, incredulous when Tawosret only shakes her head. "Okay, let's try something different." She searches through the cabinets in the mummification room in the back of the apothecary, returning to the main shop with a broken pot in her hands and places this on their table. "Try to repair this. Maybe if it is not a living being, your magic will provoke a stronger reaction in you."

Setting the pot pieces in front of her, Tiye watches as Tawosret hovers her hands over the fragments. Nothing happens at first, then the pieces rumble slightly on the countertop before they rise in the air and fly back together, restored to their original form. The only change is the slightly discolored paint, like the magic is gone.

"Did you feel anything that time? A heaviness in your limbs? A slight headache?" Tiye asks.

Disappointment stains Tawosret's face as she shakes her head.

"No problem," Tiye encourages the other woman. "Keep going. This time, we are going to try something a little more difficult."

"What do you mean by that?" Tawosret scrunches up her face, fear dancing in her eyes.

Turning her back to Tawosret, Tiye rolls up a cloth, shoving it between her teeth, tasting peppermint oil. Without giving herself time to talk herself out of it, she slams her pestle down on the top of her hand placed on the workbench. Sounds of the bones breaking in her hand mingle with the grunt muffled by the cloth. Spitting the cloth out of her mouth and between very clenched teeth, she groans, "Fuck!" before turning back to face Tawosret.

Her eyes are the size of plates as she stands rooted to the spot.

"Before you try this time, I need you to take some calming breaths because this better have been worth it," Tiye grits out.

Action coming back into Tawosret, she takes several deep breaths. Steadying herself, she takes one final deep breath before once again hovering her hands over Tiye's broken and mangled one.

The warmth is more pronounced this time as it leaves Tiye's chest, traveling down to her hand, as she feels the bones move back into place and cobble themselves together. The cold following in the wake of the warmth of Tawosret's healing is deeper. Tiye sways on the spot, gripping the workbench for support to stop herself from tumbling over.

"Anything that time?" she questions, shaking her head slightly to clear the fog.

"I am so sorry." Tears line Tawosret's eyes, her bottom lip wobbling as she talks, "I still did not feel anything in my body. The only thing I noticed was it felt as if I was maybe pulling something from the wound to heal it. Goddess please, whatever you do, don't hurt yourself again."

Flexing her newly healed hand, Tiye contemplates the implications of Tawosret's magic being unleashed to its full capacity. She needs some time to fully assess what this could mean without the weight of Tawosret's big-eyed stare. "Great work today," she says warmly. "Next time, we will practise control."

"Oh, that's it? Okay, thank you for your time and the efforts you are making to help me. Even if they are slightly deranged. We won't be doing that again tomorrow, right?" Tawosret looks worried as she speaks.

"No, I promise I will keep my deranged teaching to a minimum. Just make sure to keep yourself safe out there. Same time tomorrow," Tiye says comfortingly as she tries to hide the lightheadedness she feels. *I need to talk to Nakhtmin, immediately.*

Tawosret dips her head in acknowledgment as she pulls the creaky door of the apothecary closed behind her. Without any distractions, the adulterated doum juice taunts Tiye again from its jar on the table. Suddenly, Tiye has a wild idea.

Running across the apothecary and flinging herself out the door, Tiye sprints to catch Tawosret, stopping her when she finds her a few buildings away. She then spends several minutes convincing her to come back to the apothecary for one more test. They hurry back, Tiye practically dragging Tawosret, before locking the door once inside.

"Tiye, if you injure yourself again, I am walking out of here and leaving you to deal with it on your own," Tawosret says earnestly.

"No, you wouldn't. But I promise I am not going to injure myself again. However, as masochistic as it seems, I still believe that it was the quickest way for you to understand your magic." Tawosret narrows her eyes at Tiye, who raises her hands in surrender, talking fast, "What I want you to do is try to heal the doum juice."

Incredulity mars Tawosret's beautiful face. Yet, sighing, she does as Tiye asks without a word and hovers her hands above the jar of doum juice. At first, it looks as if nothing is happening. Then, in waves, at the bottom of the jar, the golden doum juice starts to change colors, turning a dark amber. The color change works its way upward until the entire glass is filled with the newly amber doum juice.

"Oh, my Goddess," Tawosret whispers.

"Oh, my Goddess is right!" Tiye beams back at her.

CHAPTER SEVENTEEN

Tawosret sits, leg bouncing at a table in Pepi's tavern, which is empty again, apart from Pepi and Nakhtmin, who sit at the table with her. Business just hasn't been the same since Seti took over. That, and the menu is pretty singular. Tiye worries she might have left Tawosret alone too long with her own thoughts while she went to find Senusret—who immediately finds his seat in the empty seat next to Tawosret, throwing his arm possessively over the back of her chair. Tawosret continues to stare at the table, not noticing the new arrivals.

"Do you want to explain why you dragged everyone here, Tiye?" Pepi poses.

"What are you complaining about, old man? You live and work here. I didn't drag you anywhere," Tiye retorts, although it's her nerves that are speaking.

"Well, I've been sitting here, waiting for you to get back with this chucklehead when I could have been working."

"Enough! Tiye, tell us why you have brought us here,

please." Nakhtmin's stern face shoots Pepi a look, daring him to test their patience.

"Are you still up for this?" Tiye asks, and when Tawosret's head bobs in confirmation, she proceeds succinctly, "Tawosret can heal the doum juice. Here, watch." Tiye gestures toward a glass of golden doum juice in front of them.

The trio's mouths drop open as they observe the doum juice's color shift to amber.

"Now, watch what happens to the berry," Tiye continues, taking the last berry from the bunch she gathered from the island. She places it, too, on the table in front of Tawosret.

As her magic worked, the berry fades from neon yellow to maroon, starting from the spot it touches the table and moving its way to the top closest to Tawosret's floating hands.

"The implications of this ..." Nakhtmin trails off, looking directly at Tiye.

"I know, this is dangerous," Tiye agrees. "It worked on a pot with infused paint and even me, and it pulled the magic out of me and didn't drain energy from her!"

"We need to devise an exit plan to get her out of the healer position we have put her in."

"Hello, you two. Do you want to clue in these two idiots?" Senusret says, pointing at himself and Pepi, "and the beautiful one over here, on what in the underworlds you are carrying on about? She can heal the berries and doum juice. Why are you both acting like this is a curse?"

Tiye rolls her eyes before answering, "Sen, Tawosret's magic is unlike anything I have ever seen, even other healers. Unlike my magic, which drains my energy the more I use it, when Tawosret heals someone or something, she extracts some of their magic to harness its energy for healing instead of relying on her own. The more she heals, the more magic she drains from them. It also appears that this does not diminish her energy at all. If the pharaoh or any of his guards discover her abilities, they will likely kill her."

"Bastet, this is bad! How are we going to get her out of there?" Concern etches Senusret's face, his body leaning closer to Tawosret as he takes her hands.

Tawosret finally breaks her silence, saying, "I do not want to be removed from the healer position and this not up for discussion. I know that the longer I remain there, the more information I can gather about Seti, which will aid the rebellion." She looks up only briefly so as not to be deterred. "They are even allowing me short periods of unsupervised time, already. However, if it would make everyone feel more comfortable, I will continue drinking the original doum juice to ensure my abilities do not increase, that they stay reduced … if Pepi would be kind enough to set some aside for me." Turning to face Pepi, her eyes fill with hope and determination.

Pepi nods in agreement.

Tiye is at a loss for words; the demure Tawosret has never spoken with such strength before. Nakhtmin's expression mirrors what Tiye can only assume is her own, while Senusret beams with pride.

Nakhtmin clears her throat and returns to her usual reserved demeanor. "Fine, we will not remove you from the position right now, but the moment it becomes too dangerous, or we are given even the slightest indication of danger, we are pulling you out. No arguments."

Pepi pulls the fixed doum juice toward himself, looking at it closer. "How do you want me to explain the change in color to my customers? Or do we plan to tell the village about what was in the doum juice?"

"The doum juice tastes different once it has been healed," Tiye says, demonstrating by taking a large gulp. "You could say it's a new recipe you're trying to improve its flavor. Tawosret is the only healer we have here; everyone else's magic won't be affected by the change as much. I would even advise against telling the rest of the rebellion because of the nature of Tawosret's magic, but that is your call, Nakhtmin."

"You are correct, Tiye; it puts Tawosret at too great a risk if everyone in the rebellion is aware of her ability. Pepi, please tell your customers the doum juice has changed due to a new recipe you are trying. Tawosret, do you think you are up to healing the remaining barrels tonight?"

The group watches as Tawosret heals the remaining doum juice after Pepi sets aside enough to last her until the next supply run.

CHAPTER EIGHTEEN

With the sun shining the next day, Tiye and Senusret start their trip to the island, excited for what lies ahead. Everything from the camels to the rowboat is the same at the start of the trip, except for the company. With Ahmose tucked into the scarf wrapped around her head and Senusret by her side, she anticipates that this trip will be notably different from her first.

They have been traveling for several hours, and by Tiye's estimation, they have about an hour left in their journey when the sand begins whipping their faces. Dark purple clouds roll in swiftly overhead, blocking out the sun. The sand is increasingly ripping cuts into the exposed portions of their skin, which is painful, and Tiye and Senusret hastily jump down from their camels. They rush to tie their packs to the lead of Senusret's camel before pulling Tiye's camel with the cart some distance away and burying the tongue of the cart in the sand with as much speed as they could manage. A sandstorm.

"Ahmose, you need to go bury yourself in the sand over there," Tiye says agitatedly. "You just have to get enough distance so that if I get hit, it won't kill you as well."

In response, Ahmose digs his claws stubbornly into her shoulder, lowering his body to rest entirely there, not going anywhere.

"Damn it, have those claws gotten sharper? Fine, it's on your own head." Picking up her voice to be heard above the roaring sound and distance, Tiye yells, "Hey, Sen! If something happens to me, the island is only about an hour ahead once you get across the river—"

Senusret interrupts her, shouting back over the howling wind, "Don't talk shit, Tiye. Now hunker down until we get through this, like everything else."

He curls under a thick blanket, shielding himself from the sandstorm and Tiye follows in quick succession, tucking herself in tight, Ahmose finding his spot in the crook of her neck. *We have to make it through this. We just have to*, she thinks as the storm rages.

A flash of intense, bright purple light floods the weave of the blanket, stinging Tiye's eyes. Several seconds later, a thundering crash resonates. One after another, the purple light pierces the blanket as the thundering crashes grow closer and closer. All the while, the wind and sand continue to test Tiye's grip on her covering. Her chest pounds as her sweaty hands repeatedly secure the blanket in place. A particularly bright light illuminates the space near her face, accompanied by a crackling that fills the air bouncing along her skin. There is a smell like burning hair. Almost as if in the same moment, a deafening boom rattles Tiye's ears, coming from Senusret's direction, as a fleeting scream erupts. Ice courses through Tiye's veins, every fiber of her being urging her to run to him. But she holds herself still.

As the minutes tick by, her racing thoughts drown out the remaining crashes and flashes of light as they finally begin to move further away. The wind lessens its constant tug on her covering as the flashes of purple light and crashes of sound fade away completely. Tiye makes an opening in her covering to ensure the storm has truly moved past, making it safe to leave her position. It has. Whipping off the blanket, she runs to the place where Senusret's blanket is still visible. The sand had built itself up around his shelter, burying most of his form. Ripping the blanket away from him, Tiye's heart pounds against her ribs as she assesses his body for damage.

Drowsily, Senusret pleads, "Come on, Tiye, just five more minutes of sleep."

"You utter ass! I thought you were dead!" Tiye storms away, roughly wiping away the sand crusted into every crevice of her face. Throwing herself down before the buried tongue of the cart, she shoves her hands into the sand, pulling it away as half of it cascades fervently around her hands and back into its original location. Like sand does. But the work was releasing the tension from her shoulders and trading it for a new, more useful emotion. She moves her hands as quickly as she can, reaching down until she is able to work the cart free.

"Hey Tiye, I have some bad news," Senusret says.

"What?" Tiye snarls, the sand shifting beneath her feet as she turns to face him, narrowing her eyes on him.

Senusret's hand is outstretched, pointing in the direction of his camel. Instantly, it becomes clear what the lightning struck. The camel's honey-colored hide now bears a black mark on its back, smoke still subtly rising from its form.

Tears prick at Tiye's eyes as she beholds the animal. Wishing her magic was more useful than the 'waste of energy' her mother calls it, Tiye moves to the camel. She sends her magic into it, saying, "Your sacrifice will not be wasted."

Together they mound the sand over the animal's body until he is completely buried, wiping sweat and sand from their brows as they stand.

"Obviously, I will need to ride your camel now, but you can ride in the boat on the cart," Senusret says.

"Absolutely not! I'm not the one who can shift into a wolf!" Tiye splutters. "I'm taking the camel. You can ride in the boat if you get tired." Tiye sprints away, mounting her camel in one smooth motion before Senusret has a chance to react.

Groaning, Senusret unties their packs from his deceased ride and secures them under the rowboat's transom. As he approached the space next to Tiye's camel, he transforms into his wolf form. His clothes shift into fur while his face contorts; his chin and nose lengthen as he settles onto four legs. Tiye seldom has the opportunity to see Senusret in his wolf form, but each time, she is struck by how beautiful and fierce this aspect of him is—although she has a sneaking suspicion it might be because he cannot talk this way. His coat begins as black fur on his back, fading to a warm caramel color on his belly and the lower half of his legs. His wolf form matches the size of his humanoid one, and his back reaches above Tiye's hip.

Senusret's snout dips down and then angles forward, signaling her to lead the way. After giving his camel one last glance, Tiye squeezes her legs, indicating to her camel it is time to move. Senusret trots alongside Tiye and the cart for the remainder of the journey to the shore.

The brine of the sea fills their noses as the shoreline comes into view. The sun beginning to set sends ripples of golden light across the water.

As Senusret transitions back, Tiye is amazed to watch as, just like the rest of him, his clothes return to their original form. However, she is certain that if it were up to Senusret, he would allow them to disappear upon transitioning back, just to give himself another excuse to be naked.

"Do you want to camp here for the night, or do you want to get to the island?" he asks.

"After our luck with the lightning storm, I do not want to test fate again and chance an encounter with the Ammit. Let's camp here for the night," she says.

They settle onto their bedrolls, eat their dried meat and parathas, and talk about their lives before drifting off to sleep.

CHAPTER NINETEEN

"Do you remember how to work this thing?" Senusret asks as they position the rowboat in the water.

"Yeah, it's not too difficult. Have a seat in the middle facing me."

Senusret tentatively steps into the boat, arms stretched wide and hunched low. The rowboat sways roughly side to side, then steadies. With an air of pure confidence, he swings around to sit down, but misses the seat. His body flying back, with his feet sailing over his head, he lands in the water with a giant splash. Tiye is bent double, howling with laughter until she notices Senusret has transformed into his wolf form. Sprinting up from the water, he shakes his body next to her before she has a chance to run away, sending water flying in every direction, soaking the entire backside of her clothing as she curls away from him.

"Gross! Alright, now that we are both wet, let's try this again," she says.

Senusret, back in his humanoid form, this time successfully sits in the rowboat. With him secure in his seat on the thwart, Tiye pushes the rowboat back into the water. She lands ungracefully on the keel, causing the contraption to sway from side to side, but grips the gunwale on both sides, positioning herself low and waiting for the boat to stop violently rocking. Taking her time, Tiye makes her way over to sit next to Senusret, placing her oar into the oarlock and showing Senusret how to place his.

During the time it takes them to get situated, the rowboat has drifted from their starting point. Reorienting to the location they need to get to, Tiye teaches Senusret how to use the oar. For the first several minutes, they spin in circles, each miscalculating the speed or force with which the other is stroking. Remembering the way Nebetah taught her to row, Tiye moves her hands to both oars, establishing a rhythm that provides progress across the water and thankfully, in the right direction. After a few strokes, Tiye releases her grip on Senusret's oar. Their speed increases, pushing their way across the water in no time.

Unfortunately, upon reaching the island's shore, Tiye trips when exiting the rowboat. The edge of her boot catches the lip of the gunwale, sending her body crashing into the sand as a grunt escapes her lips.

Goddesses! Dusting herself off and spitting out sand, she tests the more delicate joints for injury. Concluding she has sustained nothing significant, she remembers Ahmose was on her shoulder. Her stomach flips as she reaches up … to find him still securely in place.

Exhaling, she pulls the rowboat onto the shore, providing an easier exit for Senusret like Nebetah once provided for her. She notices he is trying to contain a smile fighting for purchase on his face. "Don't even say it."

"Say what? I am not saying anything," Senusret says with

wide smile.

The sand moves in chunks under her boots as they pull the boat fully onto the shore. Salt from the sea crusts Senusret's loose clothes now clinging to him, and Tiye is positive hers must look worse. They both turn to face the onyx-covered island.

"These boulders are very strange. Why are they so shiny?" he asks.

"I don't know, Sen, they're just strange. Maybe they have some type of magic in them" she says. For a while, the two of them just stand and stare at the ominous landscape. "Right! Let's split up to find the break in the wall. I don't know how far we traveled off course. You take that way, go no more than three hundred paces before returning to meet back here," Tiye instructs.

They each set off in their own direction, following along the rock wall. Tiye's mind begins to drift as she walks the rocks' edge, wondering what Nebetah is doing. She thinks back to the beheading she witnessed in the alleyway and questions how many other females might have been killed by the guard for Kek while they waited to come here, when suddenly she realizes she has just passed the opening.

Sprinting back to the starting position, it dawns on Tiye that she traveled further than the three hundred paces. Rounding a large boulder jutting out, Senusret comes into view, pacing back and forth, worry etched on his face.

"Sorry, I lost track of time," she flusters.

"You scared the shit out of me, I thought made the quicksand or something got you." Senusret lets out a breath, his shoulder dropping. "I didn't find the opening. What about you?"

"Yes, it is this way," Tiye says.

Starting up the path at the trail opening, they set a quick pace, the sand slipping beneath their feet as they travel.

Coming to the fork in the trail, they take the path that leads to the pool. They make a quick detour to refill their waterskins, making sure not to stand still in any particular area for too long. Then, once again head in the direction of the berry field and the pyramid.

Cresting the obsidian rocks at the end of the trail, Senusret stops in his tracks. "There are so many," he says, his mouth slack as his eyes take in the field.

"I know, the damage he could do to the magical people is terrifying," Tiye agrees. "Come on, we need to get moving; I don't want to have to stay on the shore again tonight."

Once up close, the limestone of the pyramid was rough and weathered. The massive sandstone structure is at least ten stories high, and Tiye has to crane her neck to see the top. When the trail dead ends at the pyramid, she is surprised to find it solid from corner to corner without any identifiable entrance.

Splitting up again, the pair each take one side of the pyramid. Tiye evaluates the wall of the first level, running her hands along the coarse stone as she makes her way around to the opposite side. Still meticulously scrutinizing the wall as she rounds the second corner, looking high and low for any indication of an entrance, her mind spins when she finally meets Senusret in the middle. "You find anything, Sen?"

"No, and I didn't see any other trails leading anywhere else on the pyramid."

"Okay, boost me up. I want to check out the next level."

Rolling his eyes, Senusret positions himself with his back to the wall. He bends his knees with clasped hands outstretched just in front of him. Tiye grasps his shoulders and places her foot in his hands. Once secure, Senusret shifts to a full upright position. Letting go of his shoulders, Tiye stands up straight, her eyes reaching just above the edge. The top of the first level is now in view, although it appears to be in the same worn condition as the walls, it is a solid surface.

Resting her hands on the top edge, Tiye gives it a push, thankful the wall does not budge when she tries. "I need a little more height. On three, give me a push. One, two, three."

Senusret propels her foot upward while Tiye simultaneously uses the leverage to straighten her arms. Her upper body leaning over, counterbalancing her weight, Tiye swings her right leg up over the edge to rest on the top of the first level, then rolls herself fully over the edge. She stands, shaking her trembling limbs as the adrenaline settles in her body.

She shouts down to Senusret, "You keep a lookout, while I look around to see what I can find on this level!"

Repeating the process from the ground level, Tiye works her way around the pyramid, continually testing the stones beneath her feet. The tops of the stones that make up the first level are uniform and flat, making it feel as though she is walking on solid ground. She does not discover anything to indicate an opening or anything out of the ordinary, and soon enough, finds herself back where they began their search on the ground level. In line with the path entrance below, on the wall of the second level, Tiye finds carvings decorating the wall.

"Do you see anything up there?" Senusret shouts up from his position on the ground.

"I found some weird symbols. They look like they might be letters," she says, peering harder.

Shifting and angling her head Tiye makes a closer examination of the symbols, seeing three of the twelve are faintly raised from the wall, and the indented line of a box surrounding the symbol is more pronounced than the others. On instinct, she presses the closest of the three raised symbols and, under pressure, the symbol in question indents into the wall, stilling in its new orientation. Tiye holds her breath. When nothing additional happens, she presses the next symbol to the same conclusion. Then she presses the final of the three symbols. With a metallic click, all three snap back into their original positions. *Hmmm.* Assessing that she must have used the incorrect order, she tries the symbols once more in the opposite direction of her initial test, to no avail. She tries three more combinations before the middle symbol shoots out in her direction, suspended in the air by a metal rod protruding from the wall.

Peering at the wall behind the symbol, Tiye sees that the rod is jutting out from a long oval hole reaching almost to the top and the bottom of the box where the symbol sits. She grabs hold of the symbol, pulling it down like a lever.

Nothing happens.

Tiye closes her eyes, head rolling back to face the sky, expelling a heavy sigh and in that moment, the stone she is standing on disappears from under her feet, sending her plummeting into a new darkness below.

CHAPTER TWENTY

Hanging momentarily in the air, Tiye's stomach hurtles into her throat as her body plummets. Her feet collide with something solid, forcing her legs to buckle, and sending her body flying back, ramming the entire back of her body into what feels like several solid lines. She can't tell but they seem to be equidistant. The momentum forces her body to plunge deeper into the darkness, ricocheting along the painful solid lines. Scrambling to grab a hold of anything to stop her dive further down, Tiye rolls to her stomach. Bending her leg up under herself and using her arms to hold herself in place, she comes to a stop on what she now realizes are stairs.

Moaning, she rolls back gently to rest her head and back on the surface. A clatter of hurried footsteps reaches her ears and, looking up, Tiye sees Senusret standing at the opening she just fell through.

"Tiye! Tiye, are you down there? Are you okay?" Arms stretch out wide in front as Senusret tentatively moves his way down to her location on the steps.

"Well, I found our way in," she answers, groaning as she sits up. "We need to get some light in here."

"Seriously, Tiye, are you okay?"

"I am okay, I promise. Just bruised. How did you get down here?"

"Right after you fell out of sight, the wall began moving until it formed stairs leading up to the second level, which connected with these stairs at the top," he explains.

"Shit! Ahmose!" Tiye suddenly remembers. "Are you okay? Where are you?" Lurching up to a standing position, Tiye deliberately swipes her hands out in front of her, finding a step then sweeping across it before moving to the next step. A chill settles over her skin as her hands tremble over the third step. Empty. Then, a light weight lands on her right shoulder, and the knot in her stomach unwinds, warmth spreading over her as Ahmose rubs his head under her chin.

In a soft slow voice, Senusret asks, "Did you find him?"

"Yes, he's okay," she answers with relief. "I've got him now. Let's head down the stairs. Surely there is some kind of light source down there."

Feeling for the edge of the step with her foot, Tiye takes one step down, repeating the process twice more before she reaches the bottom. Despite her hands outstretched in front of her, she manages to run headlong into a smooth surface. Her fumbling hands depress one end of the object slightly in her haste to comprehend what it is. Immediately, a sliver of blinding light bounces around the area. Tiye pushes the object more to discover that each adjustment adds more light into the area, until there is a sudden intake of breath next to her.

Turning to see what caused Senusret's surprise, Tiye's eyes widen. A long hallway with a number of circular mirrors stretches before them, each one reflecting the light from the sun originating from the mirror she was adjusting. They fill the area with light so bright, it is as if they are still standing outside. "Incredible!" she breathes.

"It is unbelievable," Senusret echoes.

Rotating to one another, smiles broadening each of their faces, Tiye and Senusret enjoy the moment before turning back. Tiye takes in the hallway once more. It contains three doors, one on each side of the hall and one directly in front of them.

"Which should we try first?" Tiye asks.

"The left door," Senusret says as he shrugs his shoulders.

Closing in on the door to the left, Tiye notices how the light flickers in and out as they move down the hall. Seizing the door handle, she depresses the lever until she hears a click. Pressing herself into the door, it holds momentarily before giving way and swinging open. Like in the hallway, light floods the room as the door is opened, unleashing reflective light from the hallway bouncing off the strategically placed mirrors inside the spacious room.

Taking in the room completely, a chill runs up her spine as bile lodges in her throat. On the right side of the room, the wall is covered with shelves filled with clear glass jars. Each jar contains an organ suspended in a clear liquid. On the left side, the wall is filled with grotesque instruments made of varying types of metal, in all shapes and sizes. But, in the middle of the room stands the most horrifying item of all. Laid out are the remains of a person strapped to a table. Their skin is mummified, clinging tightly to their bones; their face transfixed in a scream, as if even death did not give them reprieve from the agony they endured here. Not a stitch of cloth covers their body, and a metal device splays open their rib cage, revealing a missing heart.

As the thunder of her heartbeat dulls in her ears, Tiye registers Senusret talking to her. Then suddenly, he is not there, vague sounds of discomfort reach her ears but she is not listening. She hastily moves to the cabinets lining the back wall, flinging each cabinet door open until she finds what she is looking for. Tiye's eyes well with tears. *I can't leave this person like this—whoever they are—waiting for the afterlife. It isn't right.*

Extracting what she needs from the cabinets, she dumps the contents on the small, mostly empty work surface next to the table the body occupies. Pulling her dagger from her boot, she swiftly cuts the leather straps holding the remains in place. Then, carefully, she removes the bindings, tossing them aside. An examination reveals how to release the metal clamp holding the ribs spread; Tiye removes it, tossing the metal into the pile with the bindings. Making a quick slice on the left side of the abdomen, her heart sinks when she sees the cavity is empty, despite not having the correct jars with her to perform the embalming properly. Pouring water from her waterskin into a small bowl, she dips a piece of cloth into the water, then wipes the body down as gently as possible. After cleansing the remains, Tiye begins wrapping it, starting with the head, moving the remains as little as possible. By the time she reaches the shoulders, she is aware of Senusret standing across from her. With his help, they wrap the shoulders. Then she wraps the arms nearest her, before guiding Senusret through the process for the arm nearest him. After that, they work their way down the rest of the torso, legs, and feet.

"Thank you for helping me. I could not leave them like that," she whispers.

"Of course. I don't know how you do that, you know, being the embalmer," Senusret juts his chin in the direction of the remains.

"It is just part of the job at the apothecary. However, I am fortunate that people do not die too often in our village."

Looking away, water lining her eyes as heat floods her body, Tiye grabs hold of the small table, throwing it across the room with a roar. Its contents fly in every direction. "I don't understand how the magical community still supports Seti. Sure, we just found out about this, but what about the rights being taken away? What about the trees? The sand that covers the land that once held plants?" Her voice is raw, her questions pleas.

"I don't know, Tiye. I wish I could understand."

Glancing away from Senusret's pitying gaze, her eyes fall back to the mess she has made. A spark of hope rises in her chest as she notices an item on the ground mixed in with the other contents from the small table before she knocked it over.

CHAPTER TWENTY-ONE

Marching over to the pile on the floor, Tiye pulls out a leather-bound book. Opening the tome and flipping through the pages, she discovers each page is filled with handwritten notes of unspeakable experiments. Each is more despicable than the one before.

Closing the ledger, she cannot stomach looking through it anymore, she tucks the book into her bag, wiping her hands down her trousers, as if to rid herself of this horror. Determination overcomes her weariness and pain and she feels suddenly resolute, determined to find as much evidence as possible to help overthrow the pharaoh.

Striding through the doorway, a fresh pile of vomit lies near the stairs, *that must have been where Sen went when we found this room,* Tiye thinks, quickly moving past to the door adjacent. Taking a steadying breath, she rests her hand on the door handle. Footsteps echo behind her as she presses her weight into the door and pushes it open.

To their luck, when it opens, no bodies nor torture chambers meet them on the other side.

The room resembles that of an office. A large ornate wooden desk stands in the middle of the room, atop it is a metal tray bearing a strange contraption. The walls are covered in bookshelves. The majority house glass cages, each containing different types of insects, and a small portion hold actual books.

"Seriously, what is with this guy?" Senusret sidles up beside her, examining one of the glass cages with the handwritten label *Glivners*. Insect carcasses litter the bottom of the glass containers.

"He is despicable. This room is giving me the creeps. Help me look through these books to see if we should bring any back," Tiye says as she heads to the desk.

On the desk, another leather-bound journal matching the one from the first room, sits next to the strange contraption. The metal bars of the apparatus hold three circular pieces of glass, each at different heights. Each piece of glass is suspended by a different metal bar, allowing them to be adjusted into multiple configurations. Returning to the volume, Tiye opens it to find the same handwriting adorning the pages as that of the other tome stored in her bag. Flipping through, she finds its contents document experiments for creating a multitude of different insects and plants.

"Sen, check this out!" she calls him over. "This book documents the experiments that were conducted here to create different insects and plants. Most of them failed, but at least two worked. The book documents the creation of the berries growing out in the field, and the inception of the glivner. Don't you see, Seti, and most likely his healer, Kek, created the berries and the glivner."

"Do you think this is enough to take him down?" Senusret asks.

"I doubt it, because we can't prove whose journals these are. But it makes sense now why Pharaoh Eonad was so loopy and forgetful during the last campaign. I bet Seti had someone planting glivners on him." Tiye tucks the journal away with the other.

"And dosing him with the berries," Senusret muses.

After a quick perusal of the remaining books lining the room, they do not identify any others worth taking. Together, they search the desk drawers, finding only trinkets, none of which seem to provide any value to their quest. Concluding that they've uncovered all the secrets they're going to find in this room, they decide to move on to the final room, opting to come back if they have more time.

Exiting back into the hallway and making it to the final door, Tiye immediately notices something different about it compared to the others. Directly above the handle is an indented symbol of a cross with a circle nested atop it, shaped like an upside-down egg with wings sprouting from each side. Depressing the lever of the door handle, she presses her weight into the door once more, but it does not budge.

"Why aren't you opening the door?" Senusret asks.

"'Cause it is locked, smartass," Tiye hisses over her shoulder as she runs back to the second room.

Inside, she rounds upon the desk, grabbing the edge for stability and throws the drawers open once again, one by one, before seizing an item from the third drawer. Item in hand, she sprints back to the final door. The item fits snugly into the indentation. Turning the key, a circular portion surrounding the lock turns with it. Dust and grime break away from the edges of the lock as it turns in place. A heavy clunk sounds as the lock reaches ninety degrees and this time, when Tiye depresses the door handle, the door reluctantly swings open.

Gold bathes the interior. Although it is no larger than the original two rooms they've observed, the gold seems to double its appearance, bronze hues reflecting in the mirrors bouncing the light around the room. Along the edges of the room stand crates upon crates of gold coins. Golden scepters and spears are piled in a corner. Not talking, Tiye and Senusret make their way to the collection of items littering the center of the room at the base of a large golden statue. Standing closer, the statue towers over them.

Ahmose scrambles to hide in the folds of her scarf as Tiye bends down to get a closer look at the items placed at the feet of the statue. In two half-moon configurations, she finds several items strategically placed around the base of the statue. In the center of the half-moon configuration, closer to the statue, is a mummified heart resting in a golden bowl.

What magic would require a sacrifice of a heart? This cannot be good.

To the left of the heart is a branch of the berry bush, and to the right is a glivner stuck with fine long pins onto a board. In the second ring of items contained are a bundle of twined frankincense and myrrh, gold coins, remnants of dried wine lining a golden cup, a hardened paratha, a wooden dagger, and a broken pot.

Stumbling back away from the altar, Tiye falls into Senusret. "This must be an altar to the lost god Set," she says weakly.

"The god of war and chaos?" Senusret asks.

"Yes, and of storms and desert."

"Why would Seti make this altar and then abandon it?" Senusret asks as he moves around to the side of the statue. Even with his considerable height, the statue stands a head taller. Peering around it, Senusret vanishes behind it. "Hey, Tiye come check this out!"

Making her way to Senusret, Tiye comes to find him staring at the back wall. Turning, she seeing what transfixes his gaze. There, at eye level and tucked into the wall, is a safe.

CHAPTER TWENTY-TWO

"I think I've seen this shape before," Senusret says excitedly as he traces his finger over the eight-pointed star indentation at the middle of the safe. "Wait here!" Moving away, he runs out of the room and several minutes pass before he comes rushing back in, his face ashen.

"Are you okay?" Tiye asks.

"It was in the room with the ... You know, with all the torture stuff."

Not waiting for a response, Senusret turns away from her and fits the key into the safe. As he turns it, Tiye's anticipation spikes, but when the key has made a complete turn, nothing happens. Disappointment floods her system and is apparent on both their faces.

"Maybe try the other direction?" she suggests.

Senusret turns the key to the left, making a complete circle without a response from the safe.

"Did you hear that clicking sound?" he asks.

"No, I have normal ears, I did not hear any clicking sound."

Senusret rolls his eyes before his head becomes a wolf. Using his humanoid hands, he begins spinning the dial with his wolf ear pressed to the safe.

Tiye watches as he twists the key this way and that, her eyes starting to droop when a hiss and a pop come from the direction of the safe.

"You did it!" she throws her arms around Senusret, whose head has returned to its usual form.

Releasing him, Tiye scrambles around to get a look inside the safe. The safe door is slightly ajar from Senusret's machinations and shows a perfectly proportioned hollowed-out cube, just large enough to fit Senusret's head. Checking the edges for any traps, Tiye takes her time to ease the door open. She pulls it wide, light flooding into the chamber within.

Inside is a slate with bright blue lettering scrawled across it —so bright it appears to be glowing. The top of the slate is marked with the same symbol as the lock on the door leading to this room. Below the symbol, words are neatly scrawled down the remainder of the slate in the old language.

Heart hammering, Tiye feels the edges and space behind. *Ugh, please don't let there be any spiders back there.* Not finding anything, she lifts the slate out of the safe and reads words written across it.

Senusret examines it right next to her, his heavy, concentrated breathing loud in her ear. "The Dark Sun will rain destruction and chaos across the lands, the heart of a daughter born to Sekhmet can only heal, with blood and khet combined the lotus will bloom once more," he mutters.

"What in the underworlds does that mean? And why is it glowing?" Tiye asks, her scared eyes on Senusret.

They are interrupted by a new voice, cold and harsh,

"Now what have we here?"

CHAPTER TWENTY-THREE

Spinning on the spot, Tiye and Senusret find two members of the royal guard standing in the doorway, khopeshes in their hands, ready to strike at their sides.

"Put that down and turn around," says the burlier of the two, the markings on his collar defining him as the senior in rank. Turning to the younger guard next to him he says, "You know, in the ten years I've made these trips for the guard, I have never seen the opening of this pyramid. Not once."

Seizing on the distraction, Tiye whispers quick instructions to Senusret. After his slight nod, she drops the slate. Then everything happens at once. Despite being across the room, the guards lunge forward as if out of instinct to catch the slate. Senusret throws his dagger. It buries itself into the shoulder of the senior guard, sending him howling in pain to the ground.

With the younger guard distracted by his superior's fall, Tiye sneaks up behind him, slipping the wooden dagger from the altar under his chin. "Do not move or I will slit your throat."

"Please, I just joined the guard last week. I have a family," the guard whimpers, raising his hands in surrender.

His khopesh slides smoothly from his hand as Tiye removes it from him. Releasing the dagger from his neck, she side steps to face the young guard, brandishing his own weapon at him. Turning to Senusret, she says, "Nice throw. You ready to get out of here?"

"Underworlds, yes! I got a pretty witch to get back to." Senusret winks in her direction as he swiftly yanks his dagger free from the guard's shoulder, the guard's khopesh already secured at his back.

Out of the shadows, a creature lunges, rushing forward in the direction of the injured guard. It is wrapped in linen as if once mummified, the fabric now falling loose in several spots as it moves, exposing waxy, blackened skin. From its mostly humanoid form it could have once been a person, except for the branches with blood red leaves sprouting from various places.

Just as suddenly as it appears, the creature seizes the guard and bites down on his already injured shoulder.

"Ahhhhhhhhhh! Get it off me! Get it off me!" the guard yells, falling back to his knees, twisting this way and that to release the creature's hold.

The guard's screaming echoes in her ears as Tiye throws the wooden dagger still clutched in her hand. The knife makes its mark in the creature's hand gripping the guard's upper arm, and Tiye hopes it will be enough to distract it, grabbing for her other dagger.

Before she positions it, the creature lets go of the guard, unleashing a screeching noise as it bats away the wooden weapon buried in its hand. The dagger falls to the floor amidst the creature's shrieking. It claws at its wrist above the stab mark, as if trying to remove the hand altogether, jostling crates of gold coins as it stumbles backwards. Falling over one crate and crashing to the floor, it never ceases its clawing.

Tiye can only stare as its dried skin shreds from its form, its shrieks subsiding as its movements slow.

Moments later, the creature's hand, connected to its arms only by bone, bursts into flame. Fire courses up its body until it is fully engulfed. Within seconds, there is nothing but ash falling softly to the floor.

"What in the absolute fuck was that?" Tiye looks around at the others, each with wide eyes and slack jaws, still staring at the remains of the creature littering the floor. Regaining her wits, she swiftly steals the shackles and keys hanging loose on the young guard's belt, deftly locking one shackle around his wrist hanging loosely at his waist before he even registers the movement.

Muscles tensing in belated realization, his shoulders suddenly drop, and he extends his other hand to meet the shackled one.

Senusret shackles the senior guard, as Tiye grabs the wooden dagger from its place on the floor, inching further into the shadows from whence the creature came. Her heart thunders as her eyes adjust to find a recess in the wall, barely large enough for the creature to stand in. *Isis, please let this be empty.* The only exit is the trap door now recessed into the ceiling. Not finding any other hidden compartments in the room the tension in her shoulders lessens. Moving back around the altar, Tiye retrieves the slate, surprised to find it still whole. She places the slate and her dagger into her now bulging bag, securing the wooden dagger on her belt, before returning to the group.

With the younger guard in the lead, the four of them exit the room.

CHAPTER TWENTY-FOUR

Trembling from head to toe, the young guard inches his way out the door. As his full weight presses down completely onto the floor just outside the doorway, a square section below his foot sinks a few inches. Then a series of metallic clicks begin, followed by a shuddering, seizing sound overhead, and dust falls down the wall as the ceiling of the corridor starts to lower. The young guard lurches to his left, then his right, frantically whipping his head back and forth. Then he sprints forward, still cuffed, heading directly for the stairs.

"Stop!" Tiye screams, reaching out to grab him, her hand grasping air instead.

The guard ignores her warning, running further into the corridor where another portion of the floor depresses beneath his outstretched foot. He stumbles forward due to the change in height. Righting himself, the floor below him instantly vanishes, creating an opening large enough for a person to lie lengthwise in both directions. The hole is so large, it never gives him the chance to escape his fate. His strangled scream pierces the air as he plummets into the new opening. A sickening squelch echoes from the pit as his scream promptly dies, leaving a resounding silence in its wake.

No, no, no, Tiye thinks, stunned.

"Tiye, come with me, we need to grab some heavy things to use to engage any other traps," Senusret says, jolting her out of her shock.

Sprinting back into the altar room, Tiye and Senusret each grab two heavy items within the easiest reach. Racing back in the corridor, the ceiling cresting the doorways, they find the injured guard wheezing as he leans against the back wall, sweat pouring from his forehead and eyes pinned to the outside edge of the pit.

"Follow behind me exactly," Tiye says as she looks the guard directly in the eyes.

He dips his chin in mute agreement.

Tiye meticulously follows the path the younger guard took, the older guard hobbling along behind her, with Senusret bringing up the rear. Reaching the depression on the floor, she peers over the edge, bile rising in her throat as she surveys the carnage. The young guard's body is suspended in the air by nasty metal spikes running him through in multiple locations. One spike impales the base of his skull, while another pierces his chest, hitting the exact location of his heart, either of which would have killed him instantly. *This is all my fault,* she thinks.

From behind her, Senusret shouts over the clanking and clicking of the ceiling, "Tiye, can we help him? Cause we gotta go!"

Once more, Senusret's words shake her from her thoughts, bringing her back into the situation at hand. She signals no, turning away from the gruesome sight. She tosses the first of her items, a golden statue of Amun-Ra, to her right and the floor remains still. Determining that section of the floor is safe, she shuffles along the right edge of the pit, Senusret and the guard snaking along behind her.

"Fuck, that's fucked up," Senusret curses from behind her as he passes the impaled guard.

Tiye then throws a second item—a statue of Sobek—on the portion of the floor allowing passage past the pit. A section of the wall opens, firing several arrows the length of the pit, burying themselves into the wall opposite.

"Fuck!" Senusret and the guard both howl.

Tiye turns at the noise, seeing Senusret being thrown off balance by the impact of the arrow, now lodged in the outside of his upper arm, the weight of the items he is holding sends him careening over the edge of the pit. Dropping the items as he falls, Senusret scrambles to grab ahold of the edge to stop his descent.

A scream unleashes from her throat as Tiye sprints back to him, watching in terror as his fingers grasp for purchase at the edge of the pit, his left losing its grip. Throwing herself down, she latches onto his arm holding onto the edge. Tiye looks down into the pit. A spike has pierced his leg at his calf. Tiye redoubles her grasp on his arms, pulling with all of her might.

Senusret bellows in agony as the spike pulls at his leg with the movement.

Tiye faces the remaining guard, pleading, "Please help me!"

The guard does not move as he sways slightly from side to side, refusing to look at her. There is an audible crunching of metal sounds from around the room as the ceiling hits the tops of the mirrors, and the light in the room shudders. Immediately, the guard crouches, crawling his way on his hands and knees to the stairs, away from them.

"Tiye, you have to leave me!" Senusret cries.

"Absolutely not, you pigheaded fool. If you die, I die. Besides, you won't let yourself die, you have a beautiful witch to get back to. So do I. Now, quit your whining and kick your leg back off of the spike. And when you get it off, don't get it stuck again."

More crunching of metal reverberates around the room. Another mirror smashes. Licking his lips, Senusret kicks his foot up, the tendons in his neck straining, pain leashing the roar he makes as the spike slowly recedes out of his leg from his upward movement.

A mirror crashes to the ground, knocking out the light filling the back half of the corridor. Fear flashes across his face as the last of the spike disappears from his leg. With it free, Tiye gives him a heavy pull. The movement dragging him up is enough for him to rest his arms completely on the edge, the arrow still decorating his left arm. Senusret closes his eyes before resting his head on his forearms. Then a second mirror falls, sending the whole corridor into darkness, the only remaining light coming from the stairway out.

Tiye's heart makes a valiant effort to escape from her chest as an image of amethyst eyes and raven hair flashes in her mind. Sweat covers her brow as she looks at Senusret's shadowed form. "Ready, on three we are getting you out of there. One, two, three." With her arms under his armpits, Tiye pulls with all the strength she possesses.

Senusret rolls out of the pit, crashing on top of her. Rolling apart, they do not hesitate to move, carefully crawling on the floor and keeping one hand outstretched to ensure neither of them fall over the edge of the pit.

Past the pit, the ceiling has lowered to the point it is blocking most of the light emanating from the stairs.

This cannot be happening, Tiye's thoughts rage.

Moving in a crouched position on their feet, Tiye and

Senusret run side by side as best they can to the stairs. It is so low now, it is depressing Tiye's form even further into a crawl as they hit the stairs. Here, the ceiling creates a mirror image of the bottom half of the stairs she crashed down earlier and Tiye is spurred on when she realizes they only need to make it up halfway to reach safety. *Thank the Goddess we are almost there*, she thinks, just before Senusret collapses next to her. "Get up right this instant! This ceiling is not going to be the death of us!"

Without a word, Senusret resumes his crawl up the stairs, blood trailing along beside him as he moves, his breath heaving.

The ceiling presses them further down as they make their bid for escape, and hope fills Tiye's chest as she skims her ways out from the jaws of the pyramid and into the bright daylight.

Immediately turning on the steps, she pulls Senusret up the stairs. His feet clear them with seconds to spare as the ceiling seals off the bottom half leading into the pyramid. Panting heavily, they collapse back on the floor, walls surrounding them on either side as they close their eyes to the blinding sun above.

Their relief is short-lived as the light is blocked from Tiye's face. Opening her eyes, ice floods her veins.

Standing over them at the top of the stairs are two more of the creatures from the pyramid. One has a slightly taller, slimmer build, the other a shorter, more rotund form. Stained linen hangs off each of them, appearing brittle from the sun and age. Sunlight deepens red leaves hanging from the spikes protruding from their skin.

Tiye slaps at Senusret and they scramble back against the now closed wall of the pyramid with nowhere else to go; the creatures block their only exit. The things start their descent down the stairs, a clicking sound emanating from them as they move. Placing herself in front of Senusret, Tiye slashes the wooden dagger across the outstretched hand of the creature in the lead, before throwing it into the chest of the other.

Both creatures shriek after being hit, but they are not deterred from getting to their prey.

Tiye slashes the stolen khopesh at the closer creature, its blood red leaves rustling as it moves forward, ignoring the injury. Recalculating, Tiye takes a mighty swing, cutting the first creature in half with a clean slice, grateful Senusret remains behind her, leaving her the room to complete the swing. The thing's top half slides into the wall with a nauseating thud, as its bottom half falls in the opposite direction. Moving past its halves, Tiye repeats the maneuver on the second creature, but her khopesh gets stuck halfway through the creature's torso.

A tug at her ankle has her stopping her attempts to remove the weapon. To her horror, she sees the first creature has wrapped its hands around her ankle, using its grip to pull its torso up the stairs. Its mouth is open wide, serpentine tongue slithering out in the direction of her ankle.

In the next moment, a khopesh lances its head, pinning it in place on the stairs.

Looking up Tiye sees an ashen-faced Senusret releasing his grip on the khopesh's handle. He leans back against the wall again, breathing heavily.

"Look out!" a weak yell escapes his lips as he points to the second creature.

Still impaled by Tiye's khopesh, the creature has inched itself forward on the blade, pulling itself closer to her. Eyeing the dagger still buried in its chest, Tiye pulls it free, maintaining her hold of the khopesh. She slashes the creature's arms multiple times, then its face, anywhere she can reach to keep it at bay.

Shrieking and backing away, the creature shakes from side to side, attempting to get itself off the blade. But it does no good and seconds later, it bursts into flames. Heat crests across Tiye's face. Shielding her eyes, the smell of burning flesh and something acrid fills her nose. The heat dissipates as pain lances up her leg, the trousers of the ankle the creature held onto have caught fire, burning away the material. Frozen, Tiye stares wide-eyed at the flames, before a stained cloth smacks over them, flinging back and slamming into her leg again.

When Senusret pulls his tunic away from her leg once more, the flames have extinguished.

Ashes flutter around Tiye. From her position halfway up the remaining portion of stairs her eyesight clears just above where the stairs meet with the second level. She is in the perfect place to see the injured guard stumbling to the ground near the entrance of the path that will take him back to the shore.

The sight rips Tiye back into action. Looping an arm around Senusret, they make their way to the top of the stairs, then down the other side to the ground. Tiye leaves Senusret propped up against the wall, running back up to the second floor where she slams the tile still suspended in the air, back into the wall. Sprinting back down the stairs, she trips, missing the second to last step and careening into the sand below. Then, they start their slow slide back into their hiding place. Spitting the sand from her mouth, the salty, gritty taste lingering as she winds her arm around Senusret again, they head off after the guard.

A whoosh of air pushes at their backs and, turning, they see the stairs have disappeared once more, returning the pyramid to its original impervious facade.

Tiye looks to Senusret, speaking softly, "It is as if none of it even happened."

CHAPTER TWENTY-FIVE

Painfully, Senusret and Tiye quicken their pace until the guard comes into view. Blood oozes from his hip, shoulder, and leg, the red leaving a trail on the sand. He stumbles to the ground again, laboring to right himself again.

As they move closer to the guard, a shiver runs down Tiye's spine despite the heat of the day. *Something is wrong with him.* Some of the spots she previously thought were blood, are actually ruby colored leaves extending from branch-like spikes protruding from his skin. The largest of the branches sprouts from the bite mark the creature gave him. Most of his skin has darkened from its original deep bronze to an unfathomable charred color, reflective *of those creatures.* Even as she watches, pools of the new coloring start from where the leaves sprout. Tiye sees as the color spreads, covering more and more of the guard's skin, like spilled wine spreading across linen, staining every inch.

The guard falls to the ground once more, this time rolling

on to his back, impassively staring up at the sky. A wheezing-popping sound accompanies his breath. The sound of death rattling in his lungs, then his body stops moving completely. His chest sinks in, as blackened color fills his now lifeless eyes.

"What kind of magic does that? I hope to the Goddess there are not more of those things," Senusret says, shuddering.

"If there are more, I hope they never make it off this island. We need to bury him. If someone comes looking for them, we don't want them to realize we were here. If they don't make it into the pyramid they won't, if we can get him hidden."

"That's a lot of ifs, Tiye," Senusret croaks.

Giving Senusret a glare, Tiye turns in place, looking around for an adequate location to hide the body. Senusret slumps against a black boulder, panting slightly. His face is paler now than when they left the pyramid, the arrow still sticks out from his arm. Worried, she looks over it, the shaft is covered in small, serrated teeth notched into the wood. "Okay, I need you to take a deep breath. I am going to cut the fletching off the arrow."

Senusret closes his eyes in response as he leans his head back against the obsidian wall of the boulder. Tiye slings her pack around to retrieve her dagger, relief cascading over her as she spots the journals still alongside the contents of her bag. Then, she removes her dagger. Returning to Senusret's arm, Tiye grabs hold of the fletching, making a quick strike to the shaft as close to Senusret's skin as is safely possible. That leaves about two inches of the arrow exposed.

Senusret's teeth clench, muffling his yell behind them.

Placing her dagger back into her bag to free both of her hands, Tiye grips the arrowhead with one hand and the skin of Senusret's arm just below the shaft with the other. "Hey, Sen, I was thinking of asking out Tawosret. What do you think?"

Senusret's eyes fly open wide, then narrow, the territorial wolf shining through. The intensity of his eyes almost makes Tiye forget the task at hand.

"Don't you eve—"

In one swift movement, Tiye yanks the arrow free from his arm.

"Owww ... Shit. Tiye!" Senusret howls, then curses as his arm goes slack. He groans, blood dribbling from the wound, the skin left ripped and raw. "Very clever, distracting me," he says a little louder now.

"No really, I have been thinking about it—" At the look on Senusret's face, Tiye doubles over with laughter. "Your face. I can't even mess with you with that face. Don't worry, I don't have any interest in her. I'm interested in Nebetah." The image from earlier flashes in her thoughts. But before she can think more on it, a clicking sound fills the air, blasting the image from her brain.

Sweeping around, Tiye stands as a shadow looms over her. Where the guard previously lay, stands the ghastliest of creatures: black, drooling, and keen on taking Tiye down. As she turns, he moves, running toward them with a speed twice that of the creatures they faced previously.

On instinct, Tiye launches the wooden dagger. It buries itself into its chest and a clicking roar tears from its throat. He —it grabs the dagger, ripping it from his chest, and flinging it behind him. Tiye readies her khopesh.

It charges once more towards them, and Tiye slashes through its outstretched arm, knowing she cannot replicate the move from earlier. The arm falls to the ground as her swing lands, removing it just above his elbow. The creature's clicking roar reverberates the air again as it stumbles back momentarily before redoubling its efforts to get to Tiye. She shifts closer to the wooden dagger as the thing lunges for her once more, blocking her progress.

"Sen, I need your help to distract him for just a minute," Tiye pants. "I need to get that dagger."

Senusret immediately slashes at the creature's remaining arm, cutting a deep gash into it. The creature turns its sights on Senusret, lunging in his direction. A serpentine tongue whips from side to side from its mouth, as if tasting the air.

Tiye does not think any sound could be worse, until the eyes of the creature fall upon the wound in Senusret's arm, then bounce down to the one on his leg. A horrible clicking moan of satisfaction moves past its tongue as it continues to sway in the air, as if directing the creature towards the blood. Senusret pitches backwards, staggering away.

Tiye's heart drops into her stomach when she sees the creature so close to Senusret. She lunges at its back, dragging the dagger down its length, creating a deep laceration. The creature's head rears back, moments away from locking its remaining hand onto Senusret's arm. It spins again to face Tiye, roaring as it lunges at her once more. Tiye parries with her khopesh, connecting with the gash Senusret made, removing the creature's remaining arm. Swiping the dagger in two quick successions across its chest, she makes two large lacerations from shoulder to opposite hip, forming an X. Then she plunges the dagger into the underside of the creature's chin with all of her might, driving it to the hilt and sealing the creature's mouth shut.

She stumbles away, tottering over to Senusret. Clutching each other for the strength to remain standing, they watch as the stumps of its arms strain to make contact with the dagger. Deprived of warning, the creature's skin under its chin gives away from around the dagger. With its jaw freed, a roar vibrates around the weapon lodged in the roof of its mouth, as it rushes in their direction again.

"Oh, for fuck's sake! Can we not catch a break?"

Frustration lines Tiye's every word. "I am blaming this on you, I don't know how, but this is your fault," she snarks sarcastically, as she takes Senusret's khopesh with her free hand, placing herself between him and the creature.

She charges. Using the sand splitter technique Senusret taught her with her non-dominant hand, she manages to knock the thing off balance while slashing upward with the khopesh in her dominant hand, slicing through one leg.

The creature falls to the ground with a repulsive crunch, as two emerging crimson branches break off where they've begun to grow instead of arms. It begins crawling towards her using its legs and keeping its head upright, propelling itself hideously forward.

It only manages to drive itself a few more feet forward before fire erupts, engulfing it.

Tiye lunges to grab its separated limbs to add to the burning remains. Her hand is outstretched toward its leg when it too, bursts into flames. Falling back, she recoils, her hand burning from the searing temperatures. The fires extinguish almost as quickly as they started and when the heat dissipates, Tiye combs through the ashes for the wooden dagger.

Shocked it has survived once more, she pockets it, then crashes back to the ground next to Senusret, who has slid down the obsidian rock wall into a heap. Together they lie there as their heaving breaths even out.

"Well, at least we don't have to bury him now," he says weakly.

They look at each other, and a smile cracks across both their faces. Unrestrained laughter spills from both of them as they fall on the ground, sprawled out and looking up at the sky through tears of hysterical mirth.

CHAPTER TWENTY-SIX

After their laughter dies, they collect themselves, shifting the sand around the ash to disperse it. Ahmose makes an appearance as they cackle, rubbing his head against Tiye's cheek, moving to sit on her shoulder as they clean up the area. After smoothing out the remaining obvious indications of a struggle, they head back towards the shore.

Senusret's strain is more distinct the closer they come to the fork in the trail. Instinct has Tiye convincing him it's worth the detour to the small lake for more fresh water before their journey back to the village, hiding her ulterior motive to clean his wounds before any infections set in. When the water comes into view, Tiye is stunned again at its breathtaking sight.

Quickly, they make their way to the safety of the large rock she used on her previous trip to the island. After removing her bag and their boots, they both ease into the water. It is shockingly cold. The temperature first tightens their strained muscles before loosening them as they grow accustomed to it. Luxuriously floating in the water, they strip down to their undergarments, using the water to wash out the blood, sweat and grime. Satisfactorily cleaning themselves as well, they then work their way back to the rock. Despite the events of the day, the sun is only now just directly overhead as they lie on the rock, their clothes drying next to them.

Sundried and refreshed, Tiye sits up, rummaging in her bag once more. She pulls out the salve and cloth she brought with them, examining Senusret's injuries. *Thank the Goddess they do not have any redness or heat coming from around them*, she thinks. Satisfied with the cleanliness, Tiye smoothes the salve on the wounds with a nimble-fingered touch before wrapping each injury. "How does that feel?" she asks, as she sets to work on her own injury.

"Great, considering … Thanks. It feels much better since the swim."

Satisfied with her work, Tiye stores the supplies back in her bag.

"Hey, Tiye, how were you so calm back there? I mean you didn't even panic once," Senusret asks her.

"I was panicking the majority of the time," she says, frowning. "And honestly, I don't think I have ever been as scared as when you fell into that pit. But, I think probably I appear calm because of growing up with my mother. With her I always had to be on alert. I was constantly assessing, and staying calm to figure out what would end the situation. Staying calm on the outside always worked out better in the end. I guess it's become my default." Looking away, Tiye's gaze falls on Ahmose sleeping on the rock next to her, his wings reflecting glimmers of light in every direction. "I think our clothes are dry, Sen. Do you think you can make it back to the trail entrance by yourself?"

Senusret nods, noticing the direction of her gaze, and

dresses as quickly as he is able, leaving her alone with Ahmose.

"Hey Ahmose," she says gently. His neon pink eyelids disappear, revealing the black eyes behind. "Hey buddy, I am leaving." He scampers onto her palm before she can stop him and tears line her eyes as she says, "You have to stay here." Ahmose shakes his head as his claws sink into her palm. "Can't you see? It is not safe to stay with me. You have to stay here. This is your home." Ahmose's claws sink into her hand once more, as she removes him, leaving tiny cuts across her palm, placing him on the rock. She swiftly moves away, not letting herself look back, knowing this is what is best for him.

Grabbing her bag blindly and slinging it across her once more as she exits the rock, tears wet her face as she jogs to the trail opening. Wiping at them, she rounds the corner and runs headlong into Senusret. Righting themselves, they nod at each other with solemn faces before continuing back to the shore, not saying a word.

The air between them is tense as they place the rowboat into the water. Tiye is about to push the rowboat back when they spot a similar boat farther away down the shore. Registering that it must have been the boat the guards used, they pull their rowboat back to a secure spot before pushing the guard's vessel into the river, watching as it drifts away.

Back in their own boat, they push off the shore.

This day cannot end soon enough, Tiye thinks.

Their strokes are sloppy once again when they set off, sending them in circles initially. But, straightening out and establishing a rhythm, they start to make headway across the water.

At the halfway point, the reflection of the sun bounces off something in the water, blinding them momentarily. At that exact moment, Tiye's oar hits something solid. The breath steals from her lungs as realization dawns on her and she slams their oars out of the water, but it is too late.

The thing rises from the water, bringing the rowboat's back end with it, causing the front to nosedive. The motion catapults Tiye and Senusret into the sea.

Tiye plunges deep into the water, unable to stop her quick descent. She reaches out to propel herself back to the top, but even at their full extension, her arms do not break the surface. The water is thick with mud, clouding her vision as she flails about, attempting to find the way up. Her lungs burn as pressure builds in her chest.

Her heartbeat slows, as something wraps around her ankle, tugging her upwards. Tiye strains, muscles bunching as she fights the unseen hold. The pressure is a vise, unyielding. Water speeds past as it attempts to claim her bag into the depths. Forgetting her fight to release herself from the force holding her, Tiye scrambles to maintain control of the bag.

Her head surfaces, frigid water beading on her face as she gasps, the sharp scent of the sea filling her lungs. The bag's strap, slick with water, is a taut line in her grip, the bag itself is a dark shape, bobbing and swaying, just inches above the water's choppy surface. Tiye's eyes strain upward, pupils dilating as she sees her ankle held by an unseen tether, leaving her hanging upside down several feet above the murky water. A sputtering cough echoes through the thick, humid air, the sound close to where Senusret is suspended beside her in the same fashion.

Spinning in the air, the force around her ankle disappears as a new one latches around her torso, keeping her suspended over the water. She lashes her bag across her body, fingers redoubling their grip.

Tiye's heart plummets into her stomach as she takes in the gigantic creature.

It stands at least ten times her height. A long, narrow reptilian face is level with her body, with a mouth large enough it could swallow her whole. Metallic scales flash before her, shifting from a deep teal to a breezy turquoise. The shifting colors are momentarily captivating, and pull her from the present danger.

A chime-like voice, carried on the wind, reverberates through the space, "Who dares disturb my waters?"

"Who? Us?" Senusret asks.

"I am Tiye, and this is my friend Senusret. I am sorry, we did not mean to disturb you or your waters. If we promise to never return, would you let us go?" Tiye asks.

"Your promises mean nothing to me, witch. I am the devourer of souls. The weight of your soul is what will damn you."

"How are you going to weigh our souls?" Tiye asks.

"That sounds painful," Senusret says.

"We will see," the Ammit says.

In the next instant, images flash across Tiye's mind.

A memory from her childhood floods her senses. Her mother is talking to her in a sickly-sweet sort of way. 'If you do not stop crying, the guard is going to come take you away from us forever. And they will put me in the dungeons for being a bad mother. How would you feel then, knowing you were the reason I was sent to the dungeons?' Her chest tightens, a familiar pressure building in her sternum as the memory replays.

The image is replaced with her, a few years older, the headmistress is lashing her hands, glowering over her, as she says, 'You are a female, stop pretending you will be able to do anything better than a male. Now act like a female …You are an embarrassment to this school.' Her breath hitches, shallow and quick, as the phantom scent of lavender soap and cheap oils fills her nostrils, a smell inextricably linked to the manipulative words.

A new memory, Nakhtmin's family and other owl shifters of their village looking on as they lose their homes. They huddle together as the trees on the edge of the village are cut down by the royal guard and loaded into carts to be taken away to the Royal City.

The image dissolves, unveiling notices plastered on the weathered brick of village buildings. The stark black ink of the decrees of Famsastu stood out: Females are forbidden from living on their own, and marriages between witches and shifters are outlawed. A chill, like ice, crawls across Tiye's skin, prompting goosebumps and a desperate urge to flee the looming danger.

Freshly printed notices are pasted over the old ones. Her chest burns with heat as she rereads the flyer, announcing that women cannot control their own finances without a petition, and marriage between same genders is banned.

Bile rises in Tiye's throat as the next image forms in her mind. She is twenty now, the headmistress walks into the shop for a healing tincture. She scoffs between coughs, 'Surely even you could not mess this up.' The rage from the memory floods to the forefront as she feels its intention flowing into the tincture. Tiye squeezes her eyes shut, but it fails to stop the memory from inundating her mind's eye, as she sees herself two weeks later, standing off in the distance, at a funeral.

Shame floods her before the image is replaced once more. She is thirty-two, her father's face is red, his veins bulging, bearing down on her, spit flying as he shouts, 'Your only worth to this family is your marriage potential.' Her hands clench into fists, nails digging into her palms, a physical manifestation of the internal struggle to contain that rising fear and rage.

Then the fear laces her bones as she relives the scene from

the alleyway in the Royal City, followed by the scenes unfolding from the pyramid.

Tiye screams, knowing all too well what image will come next, as the memory of her leaving Ahmose behind, tears her heart in half once more. Tears cloud her eyes as the image recedes.

For a while, there is nothing.

Slowly, Tiye comes back to herself as she feels her body move in the air, the blood pooling in her head.

It is then that the Ammit speaks, "You both have shown your souls balance the scales of justice, if only just. Let your khopesh continue to know Ma'at."

Without another word, the invisible force glides them through the air and sets them gently on the shore before releasing them. They stumble but manage to stay on their feet.

CHAPTER TWENTY-SEVEN

Tiye's heart still feels heavy as they arrive where the camel was. Confusion clouds her mind momentarily looking upon the rowboat, haphazardly tossed on the cart. An oar spears the ground beside it and the other lies splintered within the hull. Shaking her head to clear her thoughts, Tiye secures the rowboat properly onto the cart, positioning their packs inside. Tiye surveys Senusret whose color has mostly returned, but the dunk in the water and the trek back to the camel have regressed the progress the water made.

"How are your wounds feeling?" she asks.

"I'll live. I think the soul weight test caused more damage," he says and his whole body shivers. "I saw the worst memories. How 'bout you?"

Tiye ignores his question. "You rest in the boat on the trip back." Grabbing a rolled paratha and dried meat for each of them, she is grateful they left their bag with the cart as she hands half to Senusret. Wishing, not for the first time, to have move variety in their meals she sighs at *paratha, again*, but the lack of water limits their land's food choices. Paratha it is. Ripping off a piece of the dried lamb in her teeth, she chews the stale meat as she opens her soaking bag. Slowly, she pulls its contents out one by one. Unsurprisingly, finding the remaining cloth soaked, she tosses it to the bottom of the boat. Grabbing the salve next, discovering it still sealed, she sets it on the transom. Next comes her dagger, placing it with the tincture before reaching back in for the journals. They are as dry as they were when Tiye first picked them up.

"How are those things still dry?" Senusret asks.

"There must be magic protecting them," Tiye says, eyeing them as she turns them over in her hands. Adding them to the growing pile on the transom, Tiye turns her bag over, dumping the remaining water out onto the ground. Something neon pink comes flying out of the bag, zooming straight to her face. "Seriously! What are you doing here!?"

As if in answer, Ahmose lands on her shoulder and rubs his head under her chin. Her heart feels like it is expanding in her chest as warmth saturates her body.

"Well now the gang's back together, you wanna head back home? I got a healer to see." Senusret's wink looks more like a grimace as he pushes himself into the rowboat.

He settles back into the packs with heaving breaths, as Tiye mounts her camel with Ahmose tucked into her scarf, once more at her neck. Squeezing her heels into the camel's side, they set off on their journey home.

The sun cresting overhead dries their clothes as they travel. The wind picks up as they continue their trek home, blasting sand across exposed skin. Verifying Senusret has already wrapped his face, she faces forward, securing her own wrapping, leaving only her eyes exposed.

As the sun sets, Tiye estimates there is only an hour left in their trip, exhaustion increasing its weight on her bones.

Landmarks of the village come into view in the distance as the wind finally ceases its relentless skin-peeling pursuit, dropping to almost nonexistence. Darkness settling in brings a reprieve to her sun-warmed skin for the remainder of the journey.

Her bones creak as she slides down from the camel when they pull up to the back entrance of the tavern. *I haven't even settled yet and I already feel old.* Tiye secures the camel to the post out back, returning to help Senusret out of the boat. "Head inside, but wait for me there. I'll grab the stuff and then come meet you to switch out the bandages. That will hold you off until you meet up with Tawosret," she says.

Senusret takes quick, shallow breaths as he nods, and stiffly walks inside with only the slightest limp. Packs slung over her shoulder, she heads inside after unhooking the cart from the camel. Using the back door, Tiye spots Pepi's safe as she moves through the back room. She unlocks it, finding it empty.

A sharp pain shoots through her finger as she reaches her hand in her bag for the journals. cutting herself on the dagger. *Ow*, she thinks crossly as she sucks a bloody finger. Carefully, she reaches in and takes out the journals.

Moving to place them inside the safe, the new crimson stains blighting the edges of the books stop her movement. Examining them, Tiye finds her blood has stained the edges of both journals. Exhaustion plaguing her mind, she shakes her head, placing them inside the safe, and leaves that mystery for tomorrow. Pulling the wooden dagger from her belt and placing it on top of the journals, she moves to shut the safe, but changes her mind at the last second. Grabbing out the dagger and tossing it into the bag with hers, she slams the safe shut.

Shuffling her way into the main room, Tiye can see the outlines of three people sitting at a table in the middle of the tavern in the dim light. As she approaches, Tawosret jumps up, running to meet her. Tiye freezes when Tawosret wraps her arms tightly around her. Over Tawosret's shoulder, Pepi gives Tiye a nod and walks into the back, leaving her captive in Tawosret's embrace.

"Oh, thank all the gods and goddesses you are alright," Tawosret says, fussing. "Sit, let me see your leg. Sen, told me you were injured too, before he fell asleep."

Dropping their packs to the floor, Tiye keeps her bag secured around her as she is guided by Tawosret into a chair. Senusret is across from her, sprawled in a chair and snoring, his head lolled to one side. Her eyes strain, searching for the rise and fall of his chest, relaxing only when the slow movements register. A slight tug at her leg her pulls her attention down and she finds Tawosret is rolling up what remains of her trousers.

She delicately unwraps the dressing, setting it aside, and examines the burn. Pulling back, she moves her arms out in front of her, hovering her palms above the charred flesh.

"Were you waiting here for us to return?" Tiye asks, trying to keep the suspicion out of her voice, something about Tawosret is not adding up.

"Oh no, I was here fixing the newest supply of doum juice," Tawosret offers, "But I must confess, I was anxious to see you both return." A blush blooms across her cheeks and her eyes dart everywhere but Tiye's face. "I like Sen very much."

Despite her suspicions, Tiye is grateful that her friend appears to have met his match. This is the last thought she has as Tawosret's healing powers pull the last of her energy from her, releasing her into a deep sleep.

CHAPTER TWENTY-EIGHT

The next morning, Tiye's muscles ache, and a new pink layer of skin has formed on her calf, framed by her deep olive complexion, it stands out quite a bit, but she doesn't mind. She dresses quickly, the rough fabric of her tunic scratching her skin. Grabbing a baladi, its warm, spiced scent filling the air, she hurries downstairs. Opening the shop door, she recalls waking in the silent tavern, a scratchy blanket draped over her. The memory of her clumsy, silent stumble home, collapsing on her bed still in her clothes, flashes through her mind.

After unlocking the front door, the sight of a lengthy order list hits her. The musty smell of old papyrus rises from the document, with the urgent rush jobs marked in hurried, red ink. Setting up her workstation, the cold metal of the tools is a cooling contrast to her skin, and she makes a mental note, *First break, I'll tell Pepi about the journals I hid in his safe.*

Tiye's not even halfway through the list of orders required

for today when the first customer walks in, needing an urgent remedy for their head pain, and thus halting her progress. The rest of the day moves by in the same fashion; she starts to make headway on the back orders and then a customer walks in. Sometimes, customers can wait for the orders, but other times not, and the poultice, tincture, tea or cream is needed immediately.

Tiye's palms thrum, her magic pulsing out as she mixes a final salve, the air thick with herbal scents. A chime echoes, it is a shrill sound, and she stifles a groan at yet another interruption.

"Be right there!" she calls and caps the glowing tincture, its label crisp, before setting it down.

Facing the intruder of her solitude, her gaze falls upon Nebetah, and the sight instantly eases the tightness in her jaw. Her lips tilt upward and her irritation is soothed like one of the very balms she is known for.

"Hey, Nebetah!" Tiye pauses there, reminding herself to breathe.

"Hey, Tiye. I am sure you are super busy right now, since you were out yesterday—"

"Wait, how did you know I was gone yesterday?" Tiye asks, inwardly chastising herself *not* to read into it. Her pulse quickens, a frantic drumbeat against her ribs. She feels a flutter in her stomach, a sensation like a thousand tiny butterflies taking flight.

"Oh, well, what I was going to say was, I wanted to see if you would be interested in having dinner with me tonight?" A slight pink decorates Nebetah's cheeks. "I came by yesterday to ask but the sign said you were gone, and would hopefully be back today."

Ah. "Of course! I would love to!" *Tone down your squeaky voice, dammit!* Tiye thinks as she clears her throat carefully. "I have to finish up here first. Where should I meet you?" Heat rises in her own face as her cheeks begin to strain. Her palms are suddenly slick with sweat, and a warmth spreads through her chest, making it hard to focus on anything other than Nebetah.

"I'll pick you up from here. I'll swing back by at closing time, then you can tell me what fun you were up to yesterday." Nebetah's onyx plait twists as she heads back out the door.

"I'll pick you up from here. I'll swing back by at closing time, then you can tell me what fun you were up to yesterday." Nebetah's onyx plait swings as she heads back out the door.

Clink, as it closes.

The color of her hair jars free a memory from yesterday before Tiye mentally bats the confusing image away. She speeds through the rest of her orders, biting her lip from time to time as she works. As she is cleaning the station, the faint scent of herbs lingers, then the door chimes. Raising her head expectantly, Tiye's face falters as she takes in the familiar elderly witch hobbling into the shop.

"Missy, can you point me to some herbs that will help with my aching back?"

"Of course, but I could whip you up something better, if you would like," Tiye says, hoping he will take her up on the offer this time. *Pleease*.

"Oh no, Missy. I want to do it myself."

Inwardly, Tiye rolls her eyes and with a slight dip of her head, she leads him over to the shelf with the dried herbs for sale.

"Can you tell me what the difference is between these two?"

Stepping into an old routine they move through each time he visits the shop, they thoroughly deliberate on six of the ten herbs when the door chime rings once more. Turning, Tiye finally gets to appreciate Nebetah walking through the doorway with a basket slung over her arm. Eyeing the elderly witch, Nebetah sets the basket on the freshly cleaned workbench.

Tiye's skin prickles as she feels Nebetah watching her while she explains each of the properties of the remaining herbs to the elderly witch. Making his selections, he hobbles his way back out the door with his purchases in hand. The sensation crawls up her spine, the hairs on her arms rising in gooseflesh as a wave of nervous energy floods her system. Her heart rate quickens and a subtle tremor runs through her hands as she tries to maintain a calm demeanor.

Nebetah watches him exit before asking, "Are you ready?"

"Absolutely, let me just change out of this quickly."

Tiye runs up the stairs, throwing open her tiny wardrobe. She picks out one of the only dresses she owns, before quickly running a brush through her hair. She makes it back down to the shop within two minutes.

Nebetah's eyes shoot up to take in Tiye hurriedly descending the stairs. "You look stunning … I have never seen you in a dress before."

"I don't wear them very often. I find them to be impractical in my day-to-day life and a general hazard with my clumsiness." The sudden compliment sends a jolt of nervous energy through her and heat climbs up her neck and face. "So, where are we going with this basket?" she says, looking away.

"I thought we could have a picnic on the edge of town, but unfortunately I could not find an adequate blanket to use—"

"Oh, I have a blanket here." Pulling the well-loved blanket she once used to sleep in the shop from its spot under the workbench, Tiye tucks it under her arm as they head for the exit.

Placing the blanket between her knees, Tiye locks the

apothecary. Then, running her hand down her thigh, inwardly curses the dress' lack of pockets as she slides the small gold key into her chest wrap. The blood seems to pound in her ears, making it difficult to focus on Nebetah's words.

They head to the edge of town, an awkwardness settling over them, and Tiye struggles to find something to talk about as they walk. Searching her brain for conversation topics, she fails to recognize the witch heading towards them.

"Tiye, is this the reason you have disgraced our family?" Sitamun eyes Nebetah up and down scathingly.

"No, Mother, please leave us be." Tiye grabs Nebetah's upper arm, pulling her down an alley and away from her mother. The muscles in her legs tighten, ready to spring into action, and her breath hitches in her throat as she steels herself to face her mother's wrath.

"Don't you dare walk away from me!" Sitamun screams.

Tiye pushes Nebetah in front of her, silently urging her forward as her heart slams against her ribs. The sound of her own breathing is extra loud as sudden adrenaline courses through her veins.

Instead of more fury, her mother cries out from behind her and, looking back, Tiye sees her on the ground, the cane she uses when her hip is acting up, lying out of her reach.

Her stomach clenches, a knot of dread forming as she sees the vulnerable figure of her mother on the ground. Tears are streaming down Sitamun's face as she reaches out uselessly in the direction of her cane. A wave of conflicting emotions washes over Tiye; guilt for her mother's pain, fear of her mother's anger, and a desperate need to protect Nebetah. Tiye whispers to Nebetah to keep moving and that she will catch up, before she moves back in her mother's direction.

Snatching the fallen cane, Tiye steadies her mother.

Firelight flickers, illuminating the alley as flames lick at her mother's hand.

Too late, Tiye steps back as a stinging slap explodes on her cheek, her own skin aflame. Stumbling, she recoils from her mother's grasp.

"You are a pitiful disgrace of a daughter," Sitamun says before she turns, limping away.

Tiye's face contorts with pain and humiliation; the burn throbs as if alive. Turning, she catches Nebetah's frozen form, her mouth hanging open slightly. Tiye closes the distance, looking down at the ground as she says, "I am sorry about that." Her shoulders slump, and her breath hitches in her throat, the air suddenly feeling heavy and thick.

"We have to get you to a healer!" Nebetah says in alarm. "Where is Tawosret?"

As if summoned by her name alone, Tawosret appears at the end of the alley. She is looking at something in her hands. From this distance, whatever it is, is concealed by the wrapping. Sensing their eyes on her, Tawosret glances up from the object, and, seeing their presence in the alley before her, she wraps the item back up, tucking it away in a pocket.

Then she sees the burn on Tiye's face and breaks into a run, closing the distance between them. "Oh, underworlds, Tiye! What happened? Can I heal it for you?" she reaches out her hands, not waiting for a response from Tiye.

"Yes, please." Tiye says breathlessly. "It was an accident," she mumbles, relief spreading through her cheek instantly at Tawosret's touch.

When Tawosret pulls her hands away, only a slight tenderness remains and Tiye lifts her hand gingerly to feel her cheek. She doesn't notice Nebetah and Tawosret looking at each other with concern. "Thank you so much, Tawosret," she says, "It feels so much better." The air smells of fresh bread and blooming jasmine, a stark contrast to the lingering fear that clung to her only moments before.

"Anytime, Tiye. I will leave you to your ..." She looks down at the basket hanging from Nebetah's arm, "picnic? I am off to see if Senusret is free." With that, she walks away without waiting for a response.

"Are you really feeling better?" Nebetah's eyes fill with pity as she looks over Tiye's face.

Her pity is a tangible weight, but Tiye pushes it away with a forced smile, desperate to salvage the evening. "Yes, I'm fine. I hope my mother did not ruin the evening." Her chin dips to avoid Nebetah's eyes.

"No, of course not. Are you still interested in picnicking on the edge town?" Hope fills her voice as she asks.

"Absolutely! Let's get there before anything else stops us!"

CHAPTER TWENTY-NINE

They manage to make it to the edge of town without further incident. Narrowly, they avoid Merneptah after Tiye spots his form. Instead, she presses Nebetah into a break in the wall with her body, hiding both of them from his sight. Peering around the corner, she waits until he disappears around the opposite corner. With him out of sight, Tiye turns her head to face Nebetah, whose shock is written all over her face. Realizing how their bodies are touching, Tiye quickly backs away, giving Nebetah space. Her flush fades as they move past the final houses.

Tiye makes quick work of laying out the blanket on the far side of a dune, obstructing them from view of the village and any unwanted gazes. With any luck, she will survive the evening without any additional embarrassment. Nebetah lays the contents of the basket out before them.

Tiye has never seen such a variety of food outside of the Royal City: two types of dried meat, four types of cheese, two parathas, and figs decorates the space between them. "This is wonderful!" she exclaims. "Thank you for putting this together."

They eat in silence for several minutes, exchanging quick glances. As they finish the meat and cheese, Nebetah remembers the wine. Pulling it from the basket with two cups, she pours them both a glass, taking a large sip. Tiye downs half of her glass, hoping it will ease her nerves.

Nebetah refills their half empty glasses, and they fall into a comfortable conversation about their childhoods while the aroma of the food still lingers. Surprised at the similarities and differences they experienced growing up in difference places, Tiye begins to relax.

Nebetah's mouth is stained with the wine and smeared with sweetness when Tiye notices a fig seed on her lip. Giggling like the girl she forgot she once was, Tiye tells her, "Oh, you have a seed stuck to your lip."

Nebetah swipes at the wrong side, missing the seed. The wine makes her forget her nerves, and Tiye leans over, balancing with one hand as she carefully wipes the seed away. Looking up into Nebetah's eyes, her heart takes off again and she promptly loses her balance, crashing into her, sending them both onto the blanket in a tangle of limbs.

Tiye's leg is sprawled across Nebetah's hips, their chests press together as they both laugh. Tiye's heart races as her eyes meet Nebetah's violet ones. Their laughter dies and their breaths mingle, each looking down at the other's lips in turn. Tiye leans closer, waiting for any hesitation or resistance from Nebetah.

As though she senses Tiye's thoughts, Nebetah's hand finds the back of Tiye's neck, pulling her down to meet her lips.

She tastes of figs and sweetness, and Tiye inhales her.

The kiss starts as a simple pressure between two mouths,

then Tiye skims her hand along Nebetah's jaw to the back of her neck. Her thumb glides up and down Nebetah's jawline, tracing the smooth skin as the kiss deepens. Nebetah runs her hand down Tiye's back in a slow caressing movement, her dress riding higher as her fingers move lower and lower.

When Nebetah slides her hand over Tiye's butt to rest momentarily, Tiye registers she has been ever so slightly rocking her hips, letting Nebetah's perfectly aligned hip create the most delicious pressure to ignite the building fire in her core. Embarrassment flits through her mind at the realization of this unconscious movement but it's forgotten when Nebetah squeezes Tiye's leg, drawing her closer, as if to remind her what they are doing.

Renewing her focus on the kiss, Tiye slides her hand down Nebetah's neck, skimming her breast, down to the dip of her waist and then back up, this time, guiding her thumb over the peaked point pressing against the tunic. She isn't sure whose moan of satisfaction reverberates in their kiss or if it comes from them both.

Nebetah's hand renews her stroking of the inside of Tiye's thigh, just shy of the wetness pooling at its apex. With her other hand, she pushes up the hem of Tiye's dress—

Tiye's head falls back, breaking the kiss with a hiss of pain. The tender burn wound from yesterday! It still hurts. Despite its appearance this morning, the injury feels like a bad sunburn when touched.

"Did I hurt you?" Nebetah asks alarmed, and sits up, causing Tiye to roll off her on to the blanket.

The cold air of the night rushing between them kills the passion in an instant, leaving Tiye feeling foolish. "No, no. I burned my leg yesterday."

"What happened?" Concern etches Nebetah's face, contradicting the glint in her eyes.

Tiye tries to comprehend. *Why is she so hard to read?* She

sheepishly explains the events of the day prior, excluding the fact that Senusret accompanied her. She is not entirely sure why she leaves him out.

A line creases between Nebetah's dark brows. "These creatures you said were on the island, they infected the guard? Turning him into one of them?"

"Yeah, they were awful. It seemed like a curse of some sort. I think it's one that Seti invented with the help of his healer. But now, we just have to prove it. Hopefully, the information will be in the journals," Tiye trails off as she thinks. "That reminds me, I need to talk to Pepi about where they are." She pauses, looking at the moon's location in the sky. "But, it's too late now."

Glancing back, Tiye notices that Nebetah appears lost in thought.

"I better head back to the Royal City," she says slowly.

Tiye's heart drops. "Oh, of course ... I had a lovely time. Are you free tomorrow night?"

"I have duty tomorrow," Nebetah says, lifting her violet eyes. "But maybe another time."

A sharp pang of disappointment lances Tiye as she nods. *Damn, I shouldn't have pushed it*, she scolds herself. Busying herself with the blanket, she takes her time to meticulously fold it as she turns her back to Nebetah.

Together, they walk back to the apothecary, Tiye carrying the basket, and the awkward silence resettles around them like a shroud. Tiye's thoughts are still racing, consumed with what could be causing the hot and cold shifts from Nebetah. As they reach the apothecary door, Nebetah leans in, handing the blanket to Tiye, and taking the basket.

She gives Tiye a swift kiss on the cheek. "Thank you for having dinner with me. Have a great night." A gentle smile plays across her face before she turns on the spot, walking into the night.

Removing the key from her chest wrap, Tiye unlocks the door. Once inside, she leans back against the wood. The sound of the lock falling into place is harsh in the quiet, the metallic scrape echoing like a scream, slicing through her thoughts.

))☾((

Tiny scaly feet with sharp talons scamper back and forth across her face, impatiently waking Tiye from a fitful sleep. With a groan, she sits up, disregarding the peculiar orange glow painting the sky outside her window, uncommon for this hour. Ahmose hovers at the door leading to the apothecary. Seeing she is up, he zooms around in laps, between her and the door.

"Alright, alright," she mutters. "Give me a minute to get dressed."

Throwing on her usual tunic and pants, Tiye opens the door for Ahmose, who instantly zips down the stairs. She works the kinks in her muscles as she ambles her way to the shop, sand cascading around her, still in her hair from last night. Scraping her fingers across her scalp, she shakes the long dark strands, freeing more sand as she shuffles her way to the workbench with a yawn.

Absentmindedly, Tiye sets up her workbench, feeling the familiar weight of each tool as she places them in their usual spot. The smooth wood of her well-worn paring knife feels cool as she grabs it, piquing sudden curiosity. She dashes back to her room, rooting around in her bag, her mind sharpening as energy courses through her, banishing the lingering fog of sleep.

Ahmose flies in circles around her every move. Tossing her bag on the bench, she pulls out the wooden dagger from the pyramid. She compares the oakwood handle of her paring knife to the wood of the dagger, the color and feel of the wood is identical. Triumph rushes through her before reality crashes her right back down. Ahmose lands on her nose, distracting her from the gloomy direction her thoughts are heading. "What has gotten into you today?" she laughs.

Suddenly, cold rushes from Ahmose, replacing the initial warmth residing on her nose moments ago. He rockets off her, landing on a scrap of linen on top of the workbench. Stone-gray coloring seeps up from his legs and belly, covering the vibrant neon pink of his scaly skin.

"Hey, Ahmose!" Tiye calls in alarm.

She reaches out for him in horror as, with slow-heavy movements, he curls into a tight ball, tucking his wings tightly into his body. It's happening so fast, Tiye is frozen with indecision and can only watch as the gray rises, his form resembling something chiseled from stone, and as Tiye stares, he is soon enveloped. She extends her hand and softly touches Ahmose, but quickly withdraws. The little creature is startlingly cold.

The apothecary door bangs open, and a male witch propping himself up on the doorway enters, panting. He looks to be about Pepi's age, but she has no way of knowing.

"Come … quick …need … embalmer," he gets out.

Tiye is momentarily torn but another glance at Ahmose reveals no change. Wrapping the linen around him, she places him in her bag with the wooden dagger she stashed as soon as the door swung open. Dashing across the room, she grabs two linen sheets and heads out the door. Tiye jogs behind the witch as he sprints down the alleys, weaving between buildings.

Her gut tightens the further they go as she recognizes the route, panic tightening her increasingly constricted breaths as they turns a final corner. Praying to the goddesses that she is wrong, Tiye follows. But the band only tightens around her chest as she skids to stop, taking in the sight.

Smoke and the smell of burnt flesh assault her senses. The fire has been extinguished, but heat still permeates from Pepi's tavern. Blackened stones crumble from where the windows once were. Tiye resumes walking over to the tavern, her insides clenching. What Tiye assumed were water witches are collapsed in a huddle not far from the building, their hair and clothes soaked. The witch who brought her here is turning this way and that until he spots her.

He jogs back to where Tiye is still rooted to the spot. "He is inside," he says. "The fire is out, but yell if you need anything. I'll be out here monitoring them. As a metal witch, there isn't much more I can do." His arms indicate the pack of water witches.

Tiye only nods, fearing what might happen if she opens her mouth. Taking a shaking breath, she walks through the burned doorway. Smoke furls from various spots throughout the tavern, as she looks around, pleading with herself, *He has to have been mistaken.*

A ray of rising sun shoots through the window, causing a glint to catch her eye and, taking in the sight, almost breaks Tiye's limited hold on her composure.

Closing the distance to the back wall, her gaze rakes over Pepi's remains pinned to the wall.

Tears brim in her eyes as she takes in the damage of his body. His arms are pinned to the wall with nails holding them out wide to each side. His lower stomach is slashed through, intestines cascading down his legs, burns encasing both. Finally forcing herself to look at his face, Tiye catches the item that caused the glint from across the room.

One of the royal guard's daggers, distinguishable by its markings, is impaled so deeply into his neck that it is buried in the wall behind him.

Fury rips through her body, sweeping out the grief, making the heat increase on her skin and, turning back to the entrance, she moves, her anger pushing her forward. At the threshold, she calls to the metal witch, explaining she needs help with Pepi, knowing she cannot get him down from the wall on her own, not with dignity.

With the metal witch in tow, Tiye heads back to Pepi's remains, the air having cleared completely now. With the absence of the smoke, the origin of the fire is now identifiable. The worst of the burns originate from the back room. Veering from her path, Tiye goes there to assess the damage. She sees the safe door is caved in, hanging open, its contents, the journals, burned to a crisp. The band around her chest constricts tighter as her head spins, and for a moment, black spots dance across her vision. Heat from the stone wall singes her palm, and she bows her head in a sudden overwhelming surge of grief.

"Hey, didn't you say you needed help?" the voice of the metal witch calls, pulling her back to the main room. "This is so awful, who would do this to him?"

"The pharaoh," Tiye seethes.

The witch's mouth drops open, then closes several times, eyes bulging as he looks at her.

At any another time, Tiye would have found it comical how the expression makes his elongated face appear like a fish out of water. But not now. Leaving him gaping, Tiye spreads out the linen sheets on the ground below Pepi, asking, "Can you do something about the nails?"

The witch nods, mouth closed but eyes still wide.

"Leave the dagger," she says.

He pulls a swig from a waterskin at his hip, then positions himself in front of Pepi. Arms wide, his hands inches away from the nails piercing Pepi's skin. He closes his eyes, wrinkles indenting his forehead as the nails begin to liquify under the direction of his magic, oozing into a dark gray puddle on the floor.

Catching Pepi's arms, Tiye gently places them to rest at his sides.

The metal witch holds Pepi's shoulder in place as Tiye removes the dagger. A harsh grating sound fills the air as she draws it, its steel blade glinting in the dim light. Wrapping it with a cloth before stowing it in the pocket at her thigh, they lower Pepi to the linens. Tiye gently arranges his organs, then wraps him completely with a top linen sheet. Using the bottom sheet, she and the witch grip a corner with each hand, slowly walking Pepi's wrapped remains suspended between them, as if they were some grotesque train.

The sun has completely risen by the time they exit the tavern. The village bustles, a symphony of clanging metal and chattering voices. People stop, frozen in their tracks, and bow their heads respectfully; everyone knew Pepi. Wordlessly, Tiye and the metal witch make their silent march past them to the apothecary.

CHAPTER THIRTY

Pepi's remains rest on the mummification table in the back room of the apothecary.

"Thank you, I can take it from here," Tiye says softly.

At those words, the metal witch speeds off with the most dignity he can muster. Everyone hates the mummification room. Most ignore it is part of the apothecary at all.

But not Tiye. Lighting the bowls of vervain and mugwort in each corner of the room, Tiye takes great care in selecting the perfect canopic jars as the herbs burn. The hazy cleansing smoke fills the air. Setting to work cleansing his body with the palm wine, Tiye's hands tremble as she unwraps the coarse linen concealing Pepi's body. She focuses on his hair or ears as she cleans his face, never looking directly into his lifeless eyes. She finds the burns only reached his legs and intestines as she cleanses the ash away from his body.

The cut across his abdomen provides her the access she needs to remove his stomach, liver, lungs and what remains of his intestine. Placing each in its own canopic jar, she leaves each one open as she mixes together frankincense, henna, and juniper. The pulsating warmth of her magic comforts her as she infuses her intention of protection and justice into the compound. She carefully divides the compound, its aroma filling the air, and places it in each jar before sealing them tightly.

Gathering more frankincense and the supple wrapping linen, Tiye approaches Pepi's head. Her trembling hands fumble so badly she has to restart the wrapping three times. Finally, she finishes the first layer. She inhales deeply, the air thick with the scent of resin, and her hands steady. Wrapping the second layer, she adds the fragrant frankincense under each section of linen, working carefully, pausing at his chest.

Rummaging through the tins lining the shelves, she can hear the soft clinking of each container holding the various items used throughout the mummification process. Crouching down, she finds the one she is looking for shoved way in the back. Popping open the lid, she reaches inside and pulls out the last blue lotus, its petals are soft to the touch.

In her fifteen years working as the embalmer for her village, she has never used the remaining blue lotus. They were rare before the drought, but since then, they have become impossible to find. Considering most people in the village die from reaching old age after they choose to settle, no one death seemed appropriate to use the sole remaining blue lotus' power of spiritual protection. Pepi's violent death is the exception.

Tiye reverently places the lotus over Pepi's heart, under the final layer of the linen wrapping.

"Tiye! Tiye! Where are you?" Nakhtmin cries from the main shop.

Grateful she has finished wrapping Pepi, Tiye calls back, "Back here, I'll be out in a moment."

Tiye is securely tucking the ends of the linen away when Nakhtmin barges through the doorway, their face stricken with worry.

"Is it him? Is that Pepi?" they call.

"Yes, it is. I was about to perform the final mummification ritual, the bowl-ringing, before coming to find you. Do you want to stay while it is performed?" Tiye asks, her voice toneless.

Nakhtmin's lip wobbles but they straighten their posture as they nod.

Gathering a large copper bowl, its dimpled walls giving it the imperfect look of perfection, Tiye places it at the head of the table with her sound wand. Replacing the vervain and mugwort in each corner of the room, she lights the herbs once more. With the smoke from the herbs wafting, Tiye takes her position before the bowl while Nakhtmin stands opposite at Pepi's feet.

Tiye gently knocks the sound wand against the outside of the bowl's opening, then smoothly rolls it along the rim. The sound reverberates through her chest, sending sound coursing out of her mouth as she hums along with the bowl.

With her next breath she sings the ritual's song, "With sound I bless your journey. You are free from harm and fear. Safe passage, beloved one. For this life will take no more." The weight of the words rest heavy on her heart, as she sings the words twice more, to ensure the power of ritual is recognized by the divine.

Before each rendition of the song, she rings the bowl. On the completion of the third chorus, power echoes encompass the room, swirling around them to match the direction she rings the bowl.

Tiye and Nakhtmin stand stoically, each focused on what remains of the person they loved, as the power stands still momentarily before the remaining sound and smoke dives into Pepi in the exact location Tiye placed the lotus. The force of the shift in the power knocks both of them forward into the table, as if it is sucking all of the energy from the room into Pepi and trying to take them along with it.

A loud *pop* sounds around the room, returning it to its dim state, and freeing Tiye and Nakhtmin from the mysterious force.

"Is that the normal set of occurrences for this particular ceremony?" Nakhtmin asks as they straighten.

"No, not with that level of intensity. I have never been pulled by the power of the ritual into the remains." Tiye ponders whether the blue lotus was the cause of the change.

Nakhtmin's hand rest on Pepi's shoulder. "Gods and goddesses shine down on you, Pepi." Silver lining their eyes, they turn away, "I will prepare the tomb at the back of Pepi's tavern for the final ritual soon, as it is almost sundown."

"Thank you, Nakhtmin. Would you like to carry him with me down to the release ritual? If not, Senusret usually helps me."

"It would be my honor." Nakhtmin gently places their hand on Pepi's wrapped cheek before turning away quickly to exit the room.

)) ☾ ((

Tiye washes herself quickly, only taking the time to add lavender, mint, and myrrh to her water basin, hoping the magic of the herbs will calm her nerves to help her get through the final ritual this evening.

Feeling calmer, she takes great care dressing in her embalmer's gown, the deep black of the silky material contrasting beautifully with the intricate golden lace design depicting the mummification process. Tiye wraps the material tightly around her waist, pinning it in place with a golden charm shaped like the head of Anubis. Next, she adds the matching bands of the material around each bicep. These depict the sacred herbs of vervain, mugwort, frankincense, henna, and juniper. Draping a plain black length of linen around her neck, she crosses the material over her bare chest, covering each breast before crossing it once more behind her back, bringing the ends back to the front to rest at her navel. Ensuring the material is smooth and the ends are even, she runs the remaining linen through the Anubis charm, securing it in place.

Mixing the henna, warmth runs down her arms as she casts the intention of strength into the compound. With the henna, she paints an elaborate design of swirling patterns and flowers, covering everything below her elbow on both arms. Deviating from the normal swirls, she paints a lotus on the back of each of her hands, covering her witch's mark.

Almost finished, she positions her arms in the beam of light streaming through the window that shows the sun's descent below the dunes on the horizon. The beams of light heat the henna, speeding the drying process and, as the last of the light disappears from the window, Tiye tests a spot on the underside of her arm. It peels away to reveal perfectly inked skin below. *Thank the Goddess! I don't think I could have sat still a moment longer,* Tiye thinks and begins to remove the rest.

Last of all, she lines her eyes heavily with kohl and affixes bright red ochre to her lips. Satisfied with the application, she places the last piece of her outfit on top of her head. Its golden band sits snugly, wrapping down to just above her ears before meeting at the back of her head. In the center of the band, a circle rises above her head, a black scarab beetle inlay on it. Surrounding the suspended circle are a pair of feathery wings flaring out around it, almost meeting at the top.

Outfit assembled, Tiye heads for the mummification room once more. She spies Nakhtmin with their hand resting on the lid of the sarcophagus whispering a final goodbye. Tiye waits silently just outside the doorway.

"Goodbye my love, I will meet you again in the underworld," Nakhtmin chokes out the words, then turns as Tiye walks into the room, tears streaming down their face. "Thank you for waiting to let me say goodbye to him alone. I have chosen to settle now that Pepi is gone. I should have done it when he asked me to but I was so focused on trying to keep the rebellion going and keep it safe. But, if I had known, I would have spent more time with him. Now all I have is the afterlife to be with him once more, and I will not wait another several hundred years to meet him there. If I settle now, I should only have to wait fifty or so years."

"I understand." Tiye rests her hand upon Nakhtmin's shoulder, her mind warring with whether she should tell them about the royal guard's dagger. Deciding against it for now, Tiye asks, "Are you ready for the final march?"

Nakhtmin nods, resolute. Kohl stains have left streaks down their cheeks, creating an almost intentional design. Dust motes dance in the sunbeams slicing through the tomb, illuminating the cool, smooth stone of the sarcophagus. Nakhtmin, their back to the massive granite, grips the cold iron bars of the platform. At the head, Tiye mirrors them, gaze fixed on the carved surface.

"Ha m djed ... Ha," Tiye commands, using the words for *ready to lift, lift*. Her voice echoes in the cavernous space.

At the ancient words, the air crackles with unseen energy and, with the command, the platform groans, the scent of aged wood and dust filling the air, and begins to lift, the sarcophagus's cold stone a palpable weight.

"Wha ... Wha" Tiye directs, *forward, forward*, her voice echoing.

At the second command, she and Nakhtmin move together through the open doors and out into the streets. They emerge, sunlight blinding after the dim room, into the bustling street. Feet pound the packed earth in unison, a rhythmic thud. They move in precise steps, making their way through the village to the tavern on the outskirts. Bowed heads line their path, whispers following. Some, drawn by the chant, fall in step, others remain rooted, until the procession passes.

With the cross street and forge in sight, Senusret comes running out, his fur beginning to sprout as he transforms into his wolf form. His padded paws fall softly onto the sand as he moves to walk beside her, matching Tiye's deliberate steps.

The presence of her best friend eases some of the strain she has been holding.

Reaching the tavern's tomb, Tiye's whisper of "Shr" barely carries, meant only for Nakhtmin's ears. *Halt.*

Together they take one step further before coming to a stop.

"Rdit r … Rdit r," she says clearly, enunciating the words for *lower.*

With the last command, the sarcophagus scrapes against the stone as it settles. Leaving the tomb door ajar, they join the crowd, the fire's heat a contrast to the tomb's chill, its light dancing in the ceremonial basin. A fire witch oversees the blaze.

"In the tradition of the release ritual we will each write a message for Pepi on the papyrus. Folding inside salt and herbs for peace and guidance. When we are all ready we will throw the messages into the fire." Tiye's voice, a deep hum, resonates as she offers the papyrus to the crowd, its surface smooth beneath the flickering torchlight, and the kohl, a cool slickness against her fingertips.

The air, thick with the scent of burning herbs, holds a quiet anticipation. With the bowl passed to the next attendee in the circle, Tiye passes the bowl containing the intention infused salt herb mixture for them to add to their completed messages. A gritty texture brushed across the skin, as each guest writes, their whispers a soft counterpoint to the crackling flames.

The papyrus and kohl are finally passed to her, and she hesitates, a lump in her throat. She is unsure how to begin, what to say. Pressure is building behind her eyes and Senusret, in his humanoid form once more, rests his hand on her shoulder, giving it a quick squeeze before handing her his message. The scratch of the kohl against the papyrus fills her ears as she quickly pens, *I love and miss you. I will not rest until I avenge you.*

Folding the papyrus, she forms a pocket, adding the sharp, salty herb mixture.

"Place your message into the fire and chant with me. *Into the afterlife, you are now free. Earthly ties are loosened from thee. To love and peace with Nephthys your soul will be.*"

Repeating the chant three times, Senusret slides back into his wolf form, howling along with the other shifters. At the completion of third rendition, the fire witch extinguishes the fire, leaving the ashes of the messages behind.

Placing her hands on each side of the basin, Tiye lifts the still hot metal as it sears her skin. Walking the basin and its contents to the tomb, she empties the ashes around the stone where the sarcophagus lies. Then, she makes a complete circle of protection with the ashes.

She offers the cool, smooth basin to Nakhtmin. The polished stone feels heavy as they receive it from her, promising a place of honor in their home. Picking up the bowl, she breathes in the sharp scent of the salt and with a resounding thud, the tomb door clicks shut. Finally, her fingers, slick with the salty compound, trace the seal.

Turning back to the mourners, Tiye proclaims, "Eat, drink, and revel. Pepi is safe with Nephthys now."

Beastly cries rip from the shifters, echoing as witch screams join in the air, a final, solemn salute. Liquor bottles are passed as the crowd sways with the music. Fire witches conjure light shows, crackling flames dancing with the wind's breath are helped by the wind witches, synced to the metal witches' heavy beats. The celebration for Pepi's life is a raucous affair.

As the night moves on, people slowly trickle off to their homes. After midnight, only the metal witch from the morning, whose name Tiye is too numb to recall, Nakhtmin, along with Senusret and Tiye herself, remain. Nakhtmin, clutching a near-empty bottle, collapses onto the sand, swaying. Taking a mighty swig, then lowering the bottle, their head slumps forward and they begin to snore.

"I can take Nakhtmin home. They live close by," the metal witch says as he walks over to Nakhtmin, "Come on, let's get you home."

They move grudgingly to a standing position, the metal witch carrying the basin as he guides them. Nakhtmin stumbles and cries, crashing to their knees several times before shifting to their owl form. Whooping, they sweep above the witch before diving into the basin, curling up in the remnants of the ash lining it.

Tiye watches with Senusret next to her. As the night went on, the intention infused bath's effects she took earlier gradually wore off. Unfortunately, her tinctures have an even shorter application time when used on herself.

Finally, with everyone's eyes off her except Senusret, Tiye collapses to the ground as the weight of the emotions she has been hiding push through the damn in her mind, flooding her every sense. Through streaming tears she wails, "This is all my fault."

CHAPTER THIRTY-ONE

"What in the underworlds, Tiye. How do you figure that?"

Wiping away the debris of the tears caking her cheeks, Tiye throws the embalmer's headdress to the side, ignoring the required reverence of the item. Deciding she does not care, she has a bone to pick with the Goddess anyway. "If I hadn't hidden the journals in his safe, he would be alive right now. The pharaoh had him killed … It was a royal guard's dagger pinning him to the wall."

"How would he even have known we took them or that they were stored in the safe?"

"Tawosret. She knew where we went and she was waiting for us when we got back. Something about her has always sat wrong with me."

"It can't be her. She hates the pharaoh more than most."

"We are talking about the same Tawosret, right? The one who gasped when I said the word fuck? You are biased; you can't help it. You're sleeping with her or at least trying to. I mean come on, Sen, she didn't even show up to release ritual."

"It just isn't Tawosret, I know it in my gut," Senusret says.

"When was the last time you saw her?"

"I haven't seen her since the night we returned from the island. I've been stuck at the forge, *making up for my absence.* If you still think it is her, first thing in the morning, we can talk to her. I know she has a reason for not attending tonight." Senusret shakes his head, rubbing the back of his neck. "Let's get some rest. I'll meet you in the morning." He shifts, taking off in the direction of the forge.

Tiye gathers all of her belongings, picking up the headdress and clutching it to her chest. Sending up another prayer, this time to the goddess Ma'at. The heat flooding her veins makes the walk back to her home a quick one. The door rattles as she slams it shut, and she takes several deep breaths before ripping the rest of the embalmer's outfit from her body. Picking up the outfit she hastily threw on her bed earlier, something tumbles out, landing on the bed.

The grey stone thuds, the chilling memory of Ahmose frozen within it instantly resurfacing. Gently, she picks him up, placing him on the bedside table. Save for his ashen hue, he appears merely asleep. Curling up, she stares, until exhaustion sends her to join him.

)) ⚇ ((

The sun has not yet risen when Tiye stirs, muscles protesting as she rolls over. A strange cracking sound pierces the stall air. Blinking the sleep and kohl from her eyes, Tiye looks around, trying to identify where it is coming from. A third crack sounds, followed by a light *plop*, pinpointing the source of the sound.

Eyes wide, Tiye watches as the stone-like covering on Ahmose cracks in quick succession, pieces falling this way and that, revealing a rich inky color below. There is a tinkling crash of the remaining shell as it falls away and, with a full body shiver, Ahmose stretches, then walks out of the rubble. Coming over to Tiye, his face lights up with a smile.

Her lips part as she takes in Ahmose's new appearance, gone is the scaly skin, replaced by a smooth jet-black fur with a single neon pink line starting at each nostril, lining the underside of each of his eyes, traveling down to his shoulders, over his hips and down the sides of his tail, meeting at the end. The only piece of him that remains the same are his iridescent wings, flapping as they bring him to Tiye's face, rubbing the side of his face against her cheek before meeting her eyeline once more.

Warmth blooms in her chest and, closing her mouth, she brings her hand up under Ahmose's floating form. "Oh Ahmose, I thought I had lost you."

A sharp banging echoes from downstairs, ripping Tiye from her thoughts as the warmth of the sun begins to bleed into the sky.

Seriously, who the fuck is here now? Footsteps pounded as she hurried downstairs, ensuring Ahmose remained above. With a tug, she throws open the door.

"Goddess, Tiye you look like shit. Do you want to fix that," Senusret gestures to his eyes, "before we go talk to Tawosret."

"Oh, shut up, I fell asleep with my kohl on. Come upstairs while I fix this," she invites him in, rolling her eyes as she sarcastically mimics his gesture.

He chuckles as he follows her up the stairs, but it dies off quickly. A laugh moving up Tiye's throat stops at a familiar lump lodged there. She forces a smile, the weight of the movement unbearable for more than a few seconds.

Tiye changes, scrubs at her face, removing the thick kohl caked on her face. Her eyes are still puffy from the day before, and she takes a moment to line them with the black pigment once more, concealing the evidence of her exhaustion and tears. Senusret lounges on her bed with his eyes closed as if exhaustion is swamping him as well.

Ahmose zooms over to where he lies on the bed, rubbing his head on Senusret's cheek.

"Hey buddy, it is good to see you—ah!" Senusret jumps up from the bed backing away from Ahmose, his eyes wide. "What in the underworlds? Is that Ahmose?"

"Yeah, it's a long story. I'll tell you as we walk."

$$))\bullet((\;$$

After persuading Ahmose with dates to stay in her room again, Tiye grabs her bag. The rough wood of the dagger presses against her palm as she confirms it is still within, the cool stone slate of the prophecy nestled next to it. With the parathas and fragrant herbs in hand, she secures them alongside the dagger's familiar weight and the mysterious prophecy.

Tiye fills Senusret in on Ahmose freezing into a stone and then breaking what seems to have been a mould, emerging transformed, as they walk the distance to Tawosret's family home. Tawosret lives on the edge of town, opposite the carriage station, and his hand flutters to his hair at an increasing rate the closer they get to the house.

Planting himself in front of the door, Senusret runs his hand over his hair once more before smoothing his tunic. With a deep exhale, he knocks on the door.

Tiye's jaw drops slightly and her eyes bulge as she takes Senusret in. *What is he doing?*

Moments later, the door creaks open to reveal an older female, about the age of Tiye's parents. "Can I help you?"

Senusret bows, straightening as he answers, "We are looking to speak with Tawosret, please."

"Oh my, she is not here right now."

"Could you tell us where she is?" Concern etches Senusret's face.

There is movement in the shadows behind the female as the metal witch appears. "Oh dear, are you looking for Nakhtmin? He, I mean they—Goddess, I hate when I do that, were in quite a state when I left them at their home."

"Hi. Um … They are fine as far as we are aware," Tiye answers. "Thank you for your assistance yesterday. I am sorry, in all the—I can't remember your name?"

"Of course, I'm Babu and this is my wife, Fukayna. How can we help you today?" Babu asks.

"We are here to speak with Tawosret. Do you know where she is?"

"A royal guard came to pick her up the evening before the fire. The guard said she would be back within a couple of days, a week at the most, but don't worry, there was a patient at the Royal City who needed an extra healer because their condition was too much for one healer alone. Should we be worried?" Babu asks.

"No, not that we know," Senusret says. "Thank you for your time. When Tawosret returns, would you be willing to let her know Senusret is looking for her?"

"Oh, you are the male she has been talking about who works at the forge. It is lovely to meet you! That must mean that you are Tiye. We will make sure to let her know you were looking for her when she returns." Fukayna says.

)) ❀ ((

Walking away from the home, Tiye's mind races. "When is the next supply run?"

"Two days. Why?" Suspicion fills Senusret's features.

"Why don't I remember Tawosret until a couple of years ago?" Tiye asks, her mind churning.

"Tawosret said her parents moved to the village right before she was born, they wanted a quieter life to raise her in. Once they saw how the schoolhouse was run, they chose to teach her at home. So, she wasn't around the village much until she started working as a healer two years ago," Senusret says.

"You don't find any of that suspicious at all?"

"No, I don't. All sorts of things influence the choices people make," Senusret says, shrugging.

"Fine, but if in two days she is not back, I am going on the supply run to figure out what is going on." Tiye answers determinedly, her torso careening forward as she stumbles over her own feet, and then rights herself once more.

"Ok, Stealthy, but that right there proves once again that you are not the best person to be spying." The Senusret smirk fights its way onto his face as they turn up the road to the forge.

CHAPTER THIRTY-TWO

The sun's intense heat beats down, amplifying the throbbing in her skull. Abandoning Senusret, Tiye trudges back to Nakhtmin's house. Her thoughts whirl as she approaches, knocking on the weathered wooden door. A resounding crash echoes from within and, moving to the window, she sees Pepi's overturned basin on the dusty floor beside the table. The door creaks open, revealing Nakhtmin's sickly green skin as they lean heavily on the handle, their face pressing against the wood.

"What?" Nakhtmin's whispers, cheeks ballooning out, their hand covering their sealed lips.

"Can I come in for a second?" Tiye asks.

Nakhtmin flings the door open as they stumble away, dropping into a couch on the opposite wall. Tiye closes the door, following them inside. Moving Pepi's basin from the floor, she places it right side up on the table, her hand and eyes linger on the rim. Tiye's breath hitches in her throat, a subtle tremor running through her fingers as if a cold wind has passed over her.

"You were like the daughter he never had, you know. He would talk about how proud he was of the person you became in spite of your parents," Nakhtmin mumbles, repositioning the arm slung over their eyes.

"He never told me that …" Tiye says, emotion forming a lump in her throat. "Thank you for telling me. I know you both had your reasons for keeping your relationship quiet but I would catch him looking at you when no one else was around. The look on his face showed how much he loved you." The muscles in her jaw clench, a visible tightening that betrays the turmoil within, and a slight flush creeps up her neck, betraying the effort it takes to maintain composure.

A glistening tear streaks down Nakhtmin's cheek and they grab for the liquor bottle. With a choked sob, they tilt the bottle back, the liquid gurgling as the last drops disappear. Tiye runs over, snatching the bottle before it crashes to the floor.

The warm, yeasty scent of cubed parathas fills the air as Tiye pulls them from her bag; she holds them out to Nakhtmin, chewing one herself. She sighs, changing up the shape does nothing to curb the monotonous taste of the flat bread.

"I do not wish to eat. Just leave me," Nakhtmin says, lying on the couch, curling their legs into their chest.

"Okay, but I will be back later to check on you again." Tiye sets the wrapped parathas on the table.

A gentle splash echoes as she fills a cup with water from the leather waterskin, its cool a contrast to the room's warmth. She sets the cup next to the food. Jotting down a note about the prophecy on the bread wrapping, she removes the slate from her bag, stowing it under the cushion of the couch Nakhtmin is passed out on.

Hopefully, this will give them something to hold onto. If anyone can, Nakhtmin can figure out what this means.

Movement outside the window pulls Tiye's gaze and she spies two royal guards marching down the sunbaked street, their polished armor glinting. Her nails dig into the soft skin of her palms as she watches them pass, the rhythmic thud of their boots fading.

Waiting until the road is empty, Tiye glances once more at Nakhtmin, then, resigned to tell them the truth about Pepi's death tomorrow, she shuts the heavy wooden door behind her as she leaves.

$))\bullet(($

Deciding it would be best for her to take the long route back to the apothecary to avoid catching up to the guards, Tiye rounds the corner of a house. Bright red lettering on the side of the adjacent building steals Tiye's focus. Moving closer, she finds herself face to face with an image of herself plastered on the poster. Her pulse spikes when she takes in the words written in red, *Wanted for Murder*. Below her face in smaller writing she sees, *Tiye Asudem is wanted for the murder of Pepi Khety. If you have any information about the whereabouts of this person, contact a member of the royal guard.*

A crimson haze blurs her sight, she rips the poster from the wall, tearing it to shreds. Tiye sprints down the street, keeping light on her feet as she moves over the sand. Two blocks away from the apothecary, she peers around the corner, her breath catching. From her shadowed vantage point, she can make out a guard posted at the shop entrance. *Well, shit!* Doubling back, she heads in the direction of the stables, wrapping her scarf to conceal her face.

At the crumbling, abandoned house, Tiye grips the rough, cold stones, scaling the walls. Reaching the flat roof, she crawls, the gritty surface scraping her palms. Peering over the edge, the metallic glint of the royal guard's armor catches her eye. A low rumble of the camels and the scent of grass wafts from the stable. Rolling back, the rough roof prickles against her, and she checks her bag. It's there: a dry, fleshy mandrake root she forgot to leave with Nakhtmin.

The hilt of her dagger smashes into the herb on the roof's floor, pulverizing it with sharp, decisive crunches, the lotus forged at the top simplifying the task. Satisfied with the resulting fine dust, she rips a small section from her scarf, the sound crisp in the air. Then, she gathers the ground mandrake onto the material, and with a steady hand, meticulously moves the powder with the blade. Holding her breath as she folds the material in half, she rolls it up tightly and tucks it carefully under her chest wrap. Experimentally, she twists back and forth to ensure it does not slip with her movement.

Satisfied, Tiye verifies that the guard's eyelids continue to drop every few seconds. She surveys the area from her vantage point but does not see any additional guards. She moves to a crouch with one leg out long behind her in the center of the roof, in line with the backside of the stable. Then, body hurtling forward, she pumps her arms and legs as fast as they will manage. Hitting the roof's raised edge, she uses her momentum to use her final footstep to catapult herself across the gap.

She lands on the back corner of the sloped roof of the stable, the soft sacking fabric absorbing any sound, but the unforgiving structure doesn't give her a chance to celebrate her success, and her feet slip, sending her sliding to the edge. Kicking her legs forward once more, she makes it a quarter span of the roof when her feet lose their purchase, throwing her over the edge. Tiye's hands blindly scrabble for any break or hold, air knocking from her lungs as her waist plummets over the roof's edge. Flailing, she tries to cling on, but the material slips from her hands, propelling her to the ground.

Feet hitting the ground, her knees give away immediately, slamming her back into the ground and knocking the scant remainder of air from her lungs with a *whoosh*. Somehow, she manages to keep her head from slamming into the ground as well. Luckily, the camels inside the paddock are grunting at one another at such a volume they likely covered the noises of her fall. From her position on the ground, Tiye sees the window she is trying to enter is in line with her feet and, rolling her eyes as she stands, she suppresses the groan aching to escape.

The window ledge comes to Tiye's waist, making it easy for her to slip inside. *Well that plan was excessive.* From the inside, she hides behind the door. To her relief, she pulls the still secure roll of material from her chest wrap, carefully unrolling it to expose the mandrake powder. She peers out the crack in the door to see the guard has leaned against the wall of the paddock, his head resting on the front window ledge, lolling slightly to the side.

Tiye creeps to the back of the paddock before skimming the walls to place herself in a mirror position inside the paddock to the guard outside. Holding the linen in the cupped palm of her hand, she snakes it outside the window, cupping it to the guard's mouth and nose. He straightens for a moment, and she pulls her hand away before the powder takes effect.

As the mandrakes' sedative properties put the guard into a heavy sleep, Tiye leans out the window as she helps his body to lower into a seated position against the wall. She hopes, belatedly, she has not used too much, or he will suffer from terrifying hallucinations that come with the use of large amounts of mandrake.

Checking the coast is still clear, she opens the paddock door, the scent of sand and camel filling her nostrils. Leading one of the beasts out, she replaces the door. The guard's snores echo in the stillness. Mounting the camel, the rough saddle meets her skin, and they are off; the dunes' undulating landscape rising before them.

CHAPTER THIRTY-THREE

The ride into the Royal City takes up most of the day. A mirage, shimmering in the heat that rises from the sand, briefly leads her down the wrong path yet, finally, Tiye drains the last of the water from her waterskin as the Royal City comes into view, sure that it is truly the Royal City this time. She gives the camel a nudge to increase his speed. Entering the city far enough away from the flow of traffic at the carriage station, the travelers looked like beetles in the sand. Dropping from the camel, Tiye unhooks his lead, leaving him to roam free. The beast wanders off lazily and she wishes she had the chance to talk to Senusret before leaving, but knows the forge master would have turned her in the instant he caught a glimpse of her.

Securing her scarf that has come loose during the ride, and leaving only her eyes visible, Tiye enters the city. The sand gives way to sandy stones and the hustle and bustle of the city floods her senses. Smells from the food carts perfume the air in every direction to entice dinner purchasers and, stealing a skirt off an unsuspecting drying line, she covers her trousers. Tiye's stomach rumbles as she passes yet another food cart selling sizzling meat. Here, in the Royal City, food is plentiful. One ahead is loaded with disc-like baladi, round, buttery yellow fayesh and meat-stuffed Hawawshi, delicacies the outer villages have not seen in years. A male walks in her direction with his head in his bag, eyeing his purchases and, speeding forward, Tiye sticks her foot out, tripping him into a female purchasing parathas from the vendor. Without looking back, Tiye lifts two Hawawshis, slipping them under her skirt as she walks away in a deliberate fashion. Behind her, she hears rushed apologies.

She settles onto the warm stone of a bench, her muscles aching but her belly full. The square bustles with the murmur of the crowd, the distant clang of a blacksmith's hammer, and the scent of pungent spices. She peers out from under her dark scarf, her eyes searching for a flash of raven hair among the royal guard as they emerge from the courthouse.

The sun sets as Nebetah makes her appearance through the front doors, chatting with another guard at her side. Tiye's heart patters as Nebetah's easy demeanor as she turns down the street leading to the palace. A flush creeps up Tiye's neck, radiating heat that she can feel prickling at her skin and her breath hitches, shallow and quick. Even now, in the impossible situation she finds herself in and her head is elsewhere. Her stomach clenches, a familiar knot of nerves forming in the pit of her belly.

Smoothly moving from the bench, Tiye walks after them, keeping her distance to not raise the attention of the guard accompanying Nebetah. Nearing the palace, Tiye realizes she is not actually at all sure where Nebetah lives. With only a block to spare, the other guard peels off in the opposite direction.

Seizing her chance, Tiye sprints to Nebetah, grabbing her arms and pulling her into the shadows. Relief floods Tiye as she surprises Nebetah, yanking the scarf away to expose her face and halting Nebetah's clumsy attempt to draw her khopesh. Confusion dances across Nebetah's features.

"I need your help, the pharaoh had Pepi killed and is accusing me for it! There are wanted posters with my face on them and royal guards all over the village. I escaped without them noticing!" Tiye relates excitedly.

"Take a breath, Tiye," Nebetah says as she tucks a strand of hair behind Tiye's ear before cupping her cheek.

The touch loosens the breath clamped around her chest, and Tiye closes her eyes as she leans into it, its warmth calming her mind. Her mind is so chaotic, so full of emotion. Yet here, with Nebetah, despite all of the noise, she finds calm.

In the wake of that thought, Nebetah guides Tiye gently to the wall, pressing her weight into her. Their breath mingles and Tiye closes her eyes once more. Leaning her head forward, she brushes her lips against Tiye's. They ignite. Fire churns in her core as Nebetah presses her thigh between Tiye's. Their kisses become frantic. Lost in the moment, Tiye's heart feels lighter for the first time since Pepi's death.

Then there is a zap at her wrist, followed by a clink of metal.

Looking down, Tiye's world is rocked as she eyes a brimstone handcuff around her left wrist, its hand still pressing into Nebetah's hip. Reality slams back into her as Nebetah clumsily tries to pull Tiye's cuffed hand behind her back, attempting to roll her front into the wall she just ravished her against.

Tiye's heart hammers, her mind kicking in to high gear. *This can't be happening!* She kicks Nebetah's knee, forcing it sideways, and a sharp crack echoes as the other woman falls to the ground. With the cold metal of the handcuff biting into her wrist, Tiye sprints away, the palace's ornate carvings blurring past. Making a wrong turn, she finds herself in the empty square by the courthouse.

Breath coming in heaves, she pulls off the stolen skirt, snagging it on her bag as she does. Realizing the contents, Tiye searches the square for a hiding place and her eyes fall upon Ma'at's scales dangling from her hand held high in the air. Hurtling herself to the statue, the shirt still streaming from her hand, Tiye flings the material around it. Using the material to move her up the statue's legs, she is able to find handholds at Ma'at's waist. Throwing the material over her shoulder, she climbs the distance to Ma'at's outstretched arm and finally, grabbing hold of it with both hands, she swings her legs up to wrap around it as well.

The skirt slips free from her shoulder as her legs lock around the arm. Tiye heart sinks as she watches the material float to the ground. Voices off in the distance jar her back into action and she scoots down to the scales, swinging her legs out to perch atop one. Slinging the bag from over her shoulder, she wraps it tightly into a ball before shoving it to the bottom of the bowl sitting atop the scale.

With the bag safe, she scales her way back up the arm. Transitioning to the torso of the statue, her foot slips, throwing her body weight onto the poorly placed handhold. Sweaty fingers lose their hold before she can establish a second one and Tiye's body scrapes down the statue, nails flaying, digging into it for anything to stop her plummet. Then at the statue's waist, her fingers latch on to the medallion below Ma'at's navel and bring her drop to an abrupt halt. Tiye looks around for another hold to lower herself to, finding nothing. The hammering of feet and voices is getting louder with each moment she fails to move, forcing her hand. There's nothing else for it. Extending her arms to their maximum length, she lets her body drop.

Slamming into the stone below, her left ankle snaps, casting her sprawling on the ground. Biting back the scream of pain, she straightens, limping away on her good right foot.

"Your Majesty, that's her," Nebetah yells, pointing at Tiye running for the alley.

A force stops Tiye, in her tracks. Although she tries, she cannot move against it. Her limbs are pulled wide, as if of their own accord and she gasps as her body levitates a foot in the air. The force turns her to face her traitor, pulling her back to where the pharaoh and Nebetah stand with several members of the royal guard. Distance removed, her back slams into something solid and a gasp escapes her, the impact stealing the air from her lungs. Her heart hammers against her ribs, a frantic drumbeat echoing the fear that claws at her throat. The muscles in her jaw clench, fighting the urge to scream as misery and rage roil in her chest. A cold sweat breaks out across her brow, and the edges of her vision begins to fill with a red tinge.

"Pathetic," the pharaoh seethes at her. "You think you have any chance of overthrowing me? The sapphic slut? I did not even know who you were until Nebetah informed me. The rebellion you are a part of, is weak and useless."

Tiye strains against the force holding her like a witch-shaped star floating a foot above the ground, but it is to no avail. People have begun to arrive, filling up the streets which connect to the main square, their bodies form a pulsating, spectating crowd.

Her heart races as Pharaoh Seti glides over to her, whispering into her ear, "Let's put on a good show for the audience." His sinister grin matches the macabre glint in his eye.

Stepping a pace away, he pulls her dagger from its holder on her thigh, with impossible speed he makes two swipes down her arms, starting at her collar bone, to her elbow on each side. The force holding her frozen releases its hold on her mouth, and she lets out a scream of agony.

The scream tears from her throat, raw and desperate, as pain explodes across her skin. Her vision swims, the world blurring at the edges as a wave of heat washes over her. Adrenaline surges, making her muscles tense and tremble in a futile attempt to escape. Goosebumps erupt, prickling her skin, as a cold sweat breaks out across her forehead and her breath hitches in ragged gasps, each one a struggle against the growing tide of hurt and terror. The area where the blade met flesh now feels like it's on fire, searing pain a stark contrast to the chilling dread that claws at her gut. Her stomach cramps, threatening to expel its contents, while a cold numbness begins to creep into her extremities.

Warm blood drips down her arms, the manacle still hanging from her wrist as the remains of her tunic pool around her waist; her torso is bare except for her chest wrap. Considering how poorly this escape plan is going, Tiye doesn't think she will leave here with that intact. "You utter piece of shit, I hope the Godde—"

An unseen force shuts off her words.

"Oh no, no, no, we won't be having any of that," Seti says with a titter as he waggles his finger at her.

Running his finger on the flat edge of the dagger, he leans his head to the side as if pondering his next meal. When his face lights with joy in the next moment, Tiye's stomach drops and she strains uselessly against the force holding her. The dagger pierces her skin above her left breast. With excruciatingly slow speed, Seti drags the blade up and over her right breast in an arc, then slashes in a diagonal line, down between her breasts, before finally arcing back up under her right breast in a crude *S*.

His magic giving her use of her mouth again, Tiye bites

down, swallowing the scream clawing its way out of her. Sticky heat oozes from the cuts on her chest as her wrapping flutters to the ground. The pharaoh repeats the pattern, carving deeper this time and this time, the scream flies from her lips. She cannot hold it back as the blood pours faster from the fresh wounds, sliding over her navel and into her waistband.

Leaning forward, Seti whispers into her ear once more, "Do you think she will think you are beautiful now?"

Tiye roars into his ear, forcing his face away from her. Turning as he releases his magic's hold on her, and sending her crumpling to the ground.

"Take her to the dungeons. Oh, and this might make it easier, she seems feral," Seti's voice is smug; he has got what he wants.

Looking over his shoulder as he departs, he folds his fingers together in her direction, the force once more controlling her head. Then, flicking his fingers forward, the force slams her head into the stone behind her.

Collapsing fully to the ground, Tiye sees her blood dripping at the feet of the statue of Sekhmet before the world goes black.

CHAPTER THIRTY-FOUR

A voice shakes Tiye awake from unconsciousness. The cold ache that has seeped into her bones prevents her from falling back to sleep and she shivers, a shadow falling over her cell— a voice sends a spike of rage coursing through her body. The muscles in her jaw clench, and a hot flush spreads across her cheeks as her fists ball up. Her heart hammers against her ribs, each beat echoing the fury that consumes her. The world narrows, focusing on the figure before her, and an overwhelming urge to lash out grips her.

"Did you know I am not even interested in women?" Nebetah asks with a sly smile. "According to the pharaoh, it is a sin against the gods for a woman to lie with another woman, but I knew I could manipulate your feelings for me. The pharaoh is doing the work of the gods. And now that I have finished this wretched assignment, he is going to promote me to an advisor at his table."

Despite her fury, reason rises to the surface on Tiye's

tongue, "Don't you see now that he has gotten what he wanted? He's just going to get rid of you. You're a loose thread *and* a female. I don't know what is worse in his eyes."

"You're wrong!" Nebetah spits, her purple eyes gleaming. "He promised me an advisor seat at his table."

The dungeon door slams behind her as Pharaoh Seti saunters in beside her. His magnolia-colored tunic and matching breeches are spotlessly clean, his long flowing robe atop flawless, adorned with gold, skimming the floor as he walks. His figure contrasts sharply with the dark, dirty dungeon walls. A ceremonial dagger hangs from his hip.

"Your Highness," Nebetah states with a bow.

"What are you doing down here with this filth, darling? I hope you are not sharing any secrets."

"Of course not, Your Highness."

"Excellent, you will make a wonderful advisor. Say your final words to this impurity."

Following his direction, Nebetah faces Tiye in the cell. She barely opens her mouth as the pharaoh, with the speed of a cobra, lunges behind her, wrapping his arm around her neck and dragging his blade deeply across her throat. Blood sprays from Nebetah's neck, coating the bars of Tiye's cell and the dungeon floor, some splattering Tiye in her position at the back.

She lunges forward as Nebetah collapses to the ground near the bars, pressing against the wound in her neck to stem the flow of blood.

"You have less than two minutes to tell me what the rebellion is planning before she bleeds out," Seti says calmly. "If I believe you've provided accurate information, I will call for the healer outside the door to tend to her."

"I'm not telling you shit, you sadistic asshole!" Tiye screams at him.

"Have it your way." Seti looks at Tiye for a long moment

before turning on his heel and strolling back through the dungeon door.

Before the door slams shut, Tiye hears the trill of a familiar voice just outside the door, "Majesty, are you in need of my services?"

Tiye hears Seti's final words, "Not just now, Tawosret."

At her feet, the gurgle and choke of Nebetah as she clutches her opened throat is accompanied by the echo of a door slamming, reverberating endlessly in the dungeon.

Tears stream down Tiye's face, the bars mashing her face as she strains to maintain pressure on Nebetah's wounds from her side, all the while aware there is nothing she can do. Nebetah coughs as more blood comes pouring out of her mouth. Seconds later, she takes her last shuddering breath, the light leaving her vibrant violet eyes as pale coloring washes her skin.

Tears mix with snot and spit as Tiye screams, begging the gods to bring her back. Her lungs constrict, causing her breaths to become erratic and shallowing. Her vision blurs, narrowing her field of sight to almost nothing.

Crumpling to the floor, Tiye takes Nebetah's limp hand in hers and lies prone next to her, only the bars separating them. Quite tears stream down her face, pooling on the sandstone floor.

Hours later, the damp chill of the cell clings to Tiye as the blood and her tears dry. A sharp jerk of her hand jolts her awake. The metallic tang of blood fills the air as reality slams into her: scraping sound of guards removing Nebetah's body. Blood, thick and sticky, matts her hair and clings to her skin. Tiye crawls to the cold stone wall, finding no comfort as silent tears stream down her face and exhaustion claims her.

))◌((

The clatter of a guard's entry echoes in the stillness as he tosses stale parathas into Tiye's cell. Finally awake, tears do not come, only rage.

"You've been out for days. I was betting you'd die any minute, dirty rebel." He leers at her reproachfully.

Tiye glowers, her eyes burning. The dried blood outside her cell is gone and she realizes someone must have cleaned it.

))☾((

"Tiye ... Tiye, wake up!"

A hiss of a whisper brings Tiye to the brink of consciousness. Pain sears across her chest as she rolls towards the sound, stopping her movement as she lies on her back.

"Shit, Tiye! Oh, my Goddess, look at you. Your—Hold still, I'm going to fix it," a familiar voice says.

Warmth begins to pull from deep inside her chest to her arm outstretched, toward the bars of her cell. Tiye's eyes fly open to find Tawosret's hand hovering over her own extended hand, her ebony braids framing her face. Scuttling back into the depths of her cell despite the pain, Tiye pulls herself into a tight ball. "Stay the fuck away from me!" she cries, her voice hoarse.

"Shhh! They don't know I am down here," Tawosret pleads, her eyes darting around nervously. "Let me help you. You are clearly in pain, and those cuts look infected."

At some point, when, she doesn't remember, Tiye tied the remains of her tunic around her chest, leaving the cuts down her arms exposed. Dirt, sand and grime from the cell have coated them and, from the tightness and heat coming from the skin around them, she knows they are in the late stages of an infection. "Don't even try it. I knew there was something off about you! I couldn't figure it out, but now I know, you're with them! Traitor! Stay away from Senusret!"

"No! No, Tiye, I am not! They are keeping me here, I

cannot leave. Nebetah came to get me the morning after you and Senusret returned from the island, claiming someone urgently needed healing. Some random witch. It was obviously a distraction to get me away, keep me occupied. After I healed the witch, who only had minor injuries, she kept using veiled threats to keep me here. And I will keep going along with what they say until I can figure out how to get us out of here."

"That doesn't prove shit!"

"Fine, if I tell you the entire truth will you let me heal you?" Tawosret hisses.

Damn it, I really need her to cure this infection, or I will be dead within a week, but how do I know I can trust her? Tiye's thoughts seemed feverish, even to her. An exhaustion so deep she does not know if she can stay conscious much longer washes over and she relents. "Fine, but I am not agreeing to believe you. Talk."

"I am the daughter of Pharaoh Eonad," Tawosret says.

"Bullshit!" Tiye cries out despite herself. *Wasn't expecting that!*

"It is true. My mother was a powerful seer. She foresaw Pharaoh Seti coming to power as well as her and my father's execution. She hid her pregnancy from the public, twenty-six years ago. I am actually twenty-six, not eighteen. After she gave birth to me, she gave me to her advisor, and her husband to raise me as their own. She made them promise to hide in Khufu until after her—after my parents' execution, then to move to Ramses." A tear rolls down Tawosret's dark cheek. Wiping it away, she clears her throat. "They said she tried to save my brothers, but Pharaoh Seti's guards tracked them down and killed anyone believed to have aided their escape. Now let me heal you."

Shame burns Tiye's neck, bring warmth back in the wake of Tawosret's magic. "I'm sorry, Tawosret." She sighs heavily.

The pain from her cuts eases as the wounds stitch themselves back together. Blackness haloes her vision and before the curtain falls once more, she manages to say, "Thank you for healing me."

))●((

Later that evening, the faint scrape of tiny claws against the stone floor pricks Tiye's ears. Fearful, she straightens, eyes straining in the dim light. Then, an onyx head, body ablaze with a neon pink stripe and iridescent dragonfly wings, emerges from the shadows and Tiye's heart swells, a genuine smile cracking the dust on her face. She reaches out, and Ahmose scrambles into her palm.

"What are you doing here? You shouldn't be here; it's not safe!" her voice cracks with emotion as, as if in reply, Ahmose settles, wrapping his legs around her thumb, a soft nudge against her skin. "Oh, alright, you can stay." Muttering under her breath, she says, "It's not like I can stop you. But, the second you hear that door open, promise me you will hide." She holds him out on her palm to check he understands. His smile grows as he nods, his tongue sticking out as he does, and her heart, so battered and broken, swells. "I mean it, I can't lose you, too," she says and sniffs.

Ahmose runs up her arm and curls up at the crick of her neck, burrowing into the warmth of her body. Gently, Tiye lies back down, this time, sleep comes softly.

))●((

The next weeks drag as Tiye assesses her cell for ways to escape, finding none. However, Ahmose's constant presence brings light back into her spirit. He sunbathes on the stones when the sole window in the dungeon allows a sliver of light into her cell and Tiye finds herself smiling more, a genuine upturn of her lips that stretches the muscles in her cheeks, a sensation she hasn't felt in what feels like an eternity.

The lightness in her spirit makes her chest feel less constricted, allowing her to breathe deeper, each inhale a little easier than the last.

With growing realization, Tiye understands what she should have before; Ahmose is her familiar.

CHAPTER THIRTY-FIVE

BOOM! Tiye startles upright to the sound of an explosion. Dust rains down on her face as the stone walls tremble around her. As the next explosion hits, a stone low in her cell wall inches toward her. Scrambling closer to grab ahold of it, Tiye pulls on the stone with a force she didn't know she still possessed after surviving off stale parathas all this time. Her muscles begin to quake with the force, causing her fingers to loosen on the stone. The third explosion has Tiye redoubling her grip as the stone inches out.

With renewed vigor, the fourth explosion sends the stone sliding smoothly out several inches. Testing the sway of the stone from side to side, Tiye can sense it is close to being freed from its confinement. Adrenaline surges through her veins, her heart hammering against her ribs, and a cold sweat slicks her palms, making it difficult to maintain her grip. But the primal urge to survive fuels her movements and she hangs on. She feels a tingling sensation in her extremities, and her vision narrows as she focuses solely on the task at hand: freeing herself.

Hoping for more explosions to ease the movement but finding none, Tiye sets about inching the stone the rest of the way out. Quarter inch by excruciating quarter inch, Tiye works tirelessly. As her strength begins to wane again, Tiye feels the wall's hold on the stone give way, catapulting her to the sand-covered stone floor. The stone delivers a punch to her gut as its final action before falling resoundingly to the floor.

As the air rushes from her lungs, a searing pain lances through her abdomen and her vision swims, spots of black dancing across her sight. Her muscles, already strained from the effort, now spasm in weak protest, cramping and twisting. A wave of nausea rolls over her, threatening to send the meager contents of her stomach onto the dusty floor.

Not waiting to catch her breath, she checks for Ahmose and scurries over to the newly made hole in the wall, shoving her head straight through the opening. She is jolted to a stop only when her shoulders catch the edges. Turning to her right, she finds pitch-black darkness. A low groan escapes the jagged edges of the hole as Tiye strains and the air, thick with dust and the metallic tang of blood, prickles her nostrils. Fear claws at her throat, a tight, suffocating feeling as she twists her head into the abyss, searching for any sign of what lies beyond.

To her left, she finds a faint light shimmering off the stone walls. Slinging herself back into her cell, she pushes and prods the surrounding stones. The light flickers, reflecting off cold, rough stone, and a dull echo of her movements fills the small space. Fear and desperation war with the cold, gritty feel of the rock under her fingers and, discovering the loosest one, Tiye kicks, shoves, and pulls until it, too, moves free. Flinging herself through the widened opening, she finds herself in a narrow passageway. She wanders towards the dazzling light coming from the spot on the wall of the passageway, tentatively edging toward the opening.

Then, voices began echoing off the walls behind her.

"Close it up. He says he isn't going to use it today anymore."

The abrupt command, followed by rapid, echoing footsteps, fade into a breathless hush.

A surge of adrenaline propels Tiye forward. The blinding light offers no comfort, just a chaotic mix of fear and anticipation as the drumming of footsteps grows closer. *Fuck it*, she thinks and hurtles herself into beckoning blinding light, her foot catching on something.

A sharp, jarring pain shoots up her leg, followed by the sickening thud of impact.

"Oh, shit!" Tiye screams, shades of green enveloping her senses as she flies face first into the ground.

Air rushes from her lungs in a painful expulsion. Gasping, she sits up, scanning her surroundings, noting only the dense set of trees around her. *How in the underworlds did I end up here?* she thinks.

The forest air is crisp, thick with the scent of damp earth and something she has never smelled before … Towering trees cast long shadows, and the dim light of dusk makes the forest seem vast and unknowable.

"You have got to be fucking kidding me," says a deep voice, laced with agitation.

Looking around, Tiye sees the most beautiful man she has ever seen.

The End

AUTHOR'S NOTE

Thank you for taking the time to read my book! More fantasy stories are to come. If you would like to stay up to date on new releases and bonus material, you can sign up for my mailing list here: byadisonblack.com.

I truly hope you have enjoyed my work! If you have time, please write a review. They make all the difference to indie authors.

Yours,

Adison

Acknowledgements

There are countless people I'd like to thank for helping me complete this book. Above all, I want to thank my person. Without you, I never would have pursued my dream of finishing and publishing this book. Through the tough days and exciting ones, you've been my rock. I love you more than words can express.

I also want to thank my editor, Agatha, for not only fixing my grammar but also seeing the story's vision and asking the right questions to make it shine.

Kyla, you took my vague ideas for a book cover and created something beautiful that perfectly captures the book's mood. Thank you!

To all my friends in real life and on TikTok, I'm grateful for your support, feedback, and advice that helped make this book a reality!

www.ingramcontent.com/pod-product-compliance
Lightning Source LLC
Chambersburg PA
CBHW020637110726
47899CB00002B/807